CURIOUS MEN

He-time Tales

ROSALIND MINETT

Uptake publications

COPYRIGHT

CONTENTS

ACKNOWLEDGMENTS

Firstly I must thank the weird and wacky women in *Me-Time Tales* for somehow producing the Curious Men in this volume. I won't thank them for their interference since.

My grateful thanks to Louise Lawrence and John Lynch (author) for their preliminary reading and advice on the stories within.

The stimulus for *A Hippopotamus is Becoming* came from a workshop by the great flash fiction writer, Tania Hershman. Something animalistic and weird came into my head after that stimulating workshop, which was actually about using science in flash fiction. I know Tania's references to using an animal or insect in fiction put the hippo into my mind. I am grateful. I can't think how this story could possibly have come to me otherwise.

Another great writer, Eileen Casey (winner of a Hennessy Award, Katherine Kavanagh Poetry Fellowship, The Cecil Day Lewis Prize and The Maria Edgeworth Award) had a dream about a man changing his name by deed poll. The name he chose was so wacky it gave rise to my story *A Strange Form of Patience*, a deceptively mild title. Thank you Eileen for giving me this stimulus. There's no way I would have summoned up this story without such a stimulus.

HEALTH AND SAFETY WARNING

Consumption of *Curious Men* is best appreciated after sampling *Me-Time Tales: tea breaks for mature women and curious men* to which this is a companion volume. Traces of that book appear in this volume. This may affect the consumer's digestion of certain Curious Men.

The well-being of consumers is our primary concern.

PROLOGUE

When I finished *Me-Time Tales: tea breaks for mature women and curious men*, I knew I had to write a companion volume; some curious men vied for my attention. It's only fair that a few men have their say, even if only the curious ones.

Some of the men in this volume are curious to behold or to live with, others are curious by nature. They are of different ages, at different life stages, one or two from different countries or different times.

Annoyingly, three women from *Me-Time Tales* strayed from their own book into this, feeling a need to nose into men's doings. They insisted on commenting. I apologise for this. I should be firmer, more in charge, but, as in life, stalwart characters dominate and win through.

Let me speak first before they do, so it is the author, not her characters, who introduces the curious men to you. Looking deeply enough into a person, I find, often reveals curious habits, features, beliefs, and even feelings. The stories in this book delve into such secrets of curious men.

From a man so passionate about the inanimate we don't even learn his name, to the man who experiences such trouble with words, as well as all the bleak and bizarre men in between, I present the curious men for your attention.

The women from *Me-Time Tales* strongly campaigned to have the last word, but I resisted. Even so, as you'll learn, in the end the men did not feel they'd had their say.

MOWN DOWN

My latest woman came with a humungous bonus. I say latest, she's the fourth, and that's not many for a man of fifty. She's very nice, smiling, pretty and lives on a farm. I'm not saying it was when she mentioned her cottage was on a farm I got interested, but, yes, that was a draw. We got talking, and I found myself listening to her and asking to see her again. The descriptions of juddering down twisty paths dodging massive tractors warmed my heart. I saw her again and again, and this became a relationship.

When she first took me to her place, I envied her the vast green fields, some flat and aching to be mowed, others hilly, dividing her from houses, concrete roads and chatty neighbours, ample compensation for the ranging whippets and overbearing cows.

I was thrilled enough, driving up the stony path bracketed by rickety sheds and stray tractor parts, but the best was to come. The farm offered dog kennels, a yard with fascinating tractors: three there were, with a provenance I looked up as soon as we returned; a slope down to a pool becoming a lake, a row of horse-boxes, stables, some occupied, a good variety of trees, more fields, the main house hidden in one of them with a needy lawn surrounding it. But as we approached her cottage ... Yes! A barn! An *empty* barn, near enough. My face must have lit up because she said, 'It's lovely to see you appreciate this place.' I agreed, but in the end, I couldn't avoid admitting my interest in the barn.

My own garden is a fair size, but you can't get to it without going through the house, so I can't keep tractors there. And I don't own anything else. I mean, my parents didn't own anything else, and I inherited the home they chose. So I can't follow my passion there. But perhaps in the back of my mind, I was leading up to it. When the vacuum cleaner broke down, I took it apart and fixed it. I found this immensely satisfying. I went online straightaway to buy another vacuum described as faulty, and fixed that. It was fascinating to discover the variation in washer sizes, together with other differences in a model that, from the outside, looked much the same as mine.

Plenty of vacuum cleaners can be picked up for next to nothing when they've gone wrong. I gained several. Some were more challenging than others to repair. (I don't like that word, "repair". You don't pair a vacuum so you can't re-pair it.)

Mending faulty vacuum cleaners presented a challenge, converting my interest into an obsession. When I got to fourteen vacuum cleaners, they took up too much space, so I sold one. It was a wrench; I spent two evenings deciding which I could more easily part with. In the end, I tossed a coin. The loser (tails) went to a good home. Do you know how uplifting it is to send a formerly inefficient, ill-functioning, rejected vacuum out into the world, knowing it will now zoom happily over carpets, sucking up dirt unreached for months?

The other thirteen vacuums remained in my house and might have been joined by another had it not been for the mower packing up in the middle of a right-hand turn on my lawn. Ah, that was the day of significance. Reluctant to respond to my efforts to fix him, the mower had to come indoors. I dismantled him on the carpet. It was my virgin examination - I had never seen the inside of a mower before. What an inspiration; an education! Having mastered the vacuum challenges, I hoped even my induction might bring success. I eagerly anticipated the first cry of the reawakened mower.

You've guessed, haven't you, that the vacuum cleaners were relegated to second place; like a football team bested. Or like when a couple have a second child. It seems much newer and more interesting than the first. I remember being a little lad enjoying piggy backs and bedtime stories. But after gaining a brother, I watched his piggy backs and overheard his bedtime stories instead, and my parents' faces now turned to him at the dinner table. Here was I committing the same disloyalty, piling up the vacuum cleaners and even selling some off while the complex innards of mowers took pride of place on every surface of my living room as well as inhabiting the carpet.

How different each mower is; each with his own voice and idiosyncracies of performance! After the excitement of bringing the first mower back into operation, the local newspaper's small ads offered others that were failing to work. I'd phone immediately. Their owners were cooperative, delivering their failed mowers in the evenings after I'd returned from work. The thrill of arrivals in the dusk or dark doubled in the morning when I could see them properly. I left them in the middle of the lawn so in the morning I could dart out of bed and see them waiting for me under the window.

I bought a shed for the mowers I'd fixed, and then a bigger one as I progressed to more advanced models. I hired a neighbour's garage, but it only held the five biggest.

I had reached the point where I despaired of a way forward when I met - Helena, her name is, by the way. So now you understand my excitement when our introductory walk around the farm where she rented a cottage, culminated in the discovery of an empty barn.

It wasn't quite empty because she stored pieces of furniture there, too large for her cottage. We soon moved those to make room for the mowers. So useful that she worked from home; she could take in postal packages of mower parts during the day. Until then, I'd had to collect them from the sorting office, often a day and a half after their arrival. She kept them on top of her fridge for a while, but the pile grew too high and toppled over onto her embroidery stools (she did this for a living). She said these stools needed to be kept very clean. She can be rather a fuss-pot.

I did buy a cupboard to house my spare parts, and that should have solved the problem, but for some reason she had preferences over furniture, one cupboard regarded as superior to another in some weird way, type of wood, colour, composition? I don't know. I could only see that each held an identical amount. She moaned about the look of mine so I turned her armchair to face the opposite direction.

Further, she had preferences about which storage space was used for which item. For instance, her tea towel drawer was half empty and so I put the half-cleaned engines there to separate them from those not yet treated with 4-stroke oil. She became awkward, Helena, and was strict with me in a way I hadn't envisaged. She produced an unwanted cardboard carton for my engines, wanting them kept in the barn despite this being a four-minute walk from the cottage.

Engines were not the only parts she wanted consigned to the barn, so I found myself spending more and more time down there. As I explained to her, it was from necessity. She queried this word "necessity", differentiating my "hobby" of bringing of mowers back to life, from my paid work as a front-end developer. She called my mower activity a back-end invader. We laughed a lot at her humour. I like to think I've enriched her life. Afterwards, I showed her the little poster I had seen locally, saying, 'Look, this has given me an idea.'

When cutting the grass, lawnmowers can have a rough time with bumps in the garden and debris on the lawn. But with the help of a few spare parts, your lawnmower could last for years to come. Your repair genius will supply the care for perfect operation.

'You're not intending to offer repair services here, are you!'

I reassured her, though doing so was intensely disappointing. There's loads of room on a farm. All sorts of bits can be laid out and worked upon without anyone worrying. But she pointed out

I was not here all the time to see these laid-out bits and sections and parts, and she was; she preferred to look at her plants. I hadn't moved her pots and containers far, just enough to lay out a few mower handles whose ends needed de-rusting, but apparently this was too far for flowers to be visible from her window. Unreasonable: she could easily pop her head around the door to look at them whenever she wanted, but she could be awkward - Helena.

Also, people are funny about their preferences. I've noticed this before. I was married once. That was the second woman in my life, and she had preferences. Eventually, I wasn't one of them.

But back to positive things. Did you know that lawnmowers have individual personalities? I bought a second Zingspark Cutter, tempted by its knock-down price and its amusing manner of turning at the end of each mowing line. The next Zingspark provided the same entertainment in this respect, but had a different voice. It was less of a regular zing, zing, zing and more of a higher tsing, tsing-tsing. I over-cut the lawn, listening to it. But grass grows.

And that brings me to another wonderful bonus in having this new woman in my life. She has great friends. My favourite lives in a large flat with french doors opening onto an immense sloping lawn that would be beautiful if kept properly mown. And now it is.

Yes, it was me who rectified his lawn situation - Mar-something, his name is. He owned a scarlet sit-on mower I was delighted to do more than sit on. It was in a sad state, he being a composer with long white fingers that probably never turned a nut onto its bolt or greased a grass box quick clip knob.

He told me the engine revved and died. After explaining that this could be, often is, due to a poorly adjusted spark plug, I rapidly turned to, surgically removing its red shell to expose its failing internals. I was spurred on during the hard and probably lengthy task by imagining riding atop the growling monster as it seared the grass. It would leave velvet tips for the view of - Marcus, wasn't it? - as he wielded his pen across his staves.

Helena came out wistfully, mentioning she had known Marcus

for many years. They met for tea and spiced ginger cake, and sometimes tennis, around once a week. The tea and cake were waiting right now and there was an outside loo where it would be better if I washed off the black oil before joining them.

It was an anxious cup of tea, my eyes directed through the open french doors to the splayed sides of the mower.

'This is awfully good of you,' Marcus said, but actually his name was Marston, he informed me.

'Mast-on!' I quipped, 'better than mast off.' They both enjoyed my humour very much and I sensed it was a turn- up for Helena's book that she could now offer me when visiting, benefiting her friend with novel stimulation. Who knows, Marston might have been getting bored *right at that point in the year* with Helena's ginger cake or tennis. He may not get many visitors, or at least, not visitors like me.

After tea, I was quickly back to work. Have you ever seen inside a sit-on mower? It's quite different from one you push. Shall I explain? — Oh. Well, just the gist, then.

I could list the parts from left to right and up to down. Best to lay them out. The sprockets and washers risked getting lost in the long grass, so I called out to Marston for a spare sheet to lay the parts upon. That way they'd show up more vividly.

He explained he'd invested in some rather fine sheets. He'd rather not lend me one of them for this purpose, but, given that I was engaged in this activity for his benefit, well—his mower's benefit, a mower from whose performance he'd soon profit, he conceded he could put his hands on some banquet cloths he'd inherited and was unlikely ever to use. These turned out to be even better than his sheets would have been, featuring shiny flowers that served like receptacles separating the small items. Each flower acted as a category: wheel function, motor function, drive shaft and so on. The workings of this creature deserved my full attention. Do you know, the most fascinating part was its throttle linkage?

Some hours later, Helena brought out a lantern and a lamp and placed one on either side of me as I worked. This was a help; her guilty gesture, I think, because as the daylight failed she'd whispered to me, 'Perhaps Marston has other ideas for his evening. I normally only stay for tea-time, and actually I'm a little chilly and a lot bored with watching tractor parts.' How harsh! I suppose I hadn't known her long enough or developed our relationship fully. However, the lamp gesture mitigated against bitter repartee, even if some had come to mind during the release of the worm gear and brake level from the central portion.

A whiff of carrot and coriander and a whirl of steam preceded Marston into my aura of light.

'Soup. When you've drunk that, I'd really like you to go back with Helena and take a rest. So good of you to put in this work, but enough is enough. These parts will be safe where they are. No-one will be coming here and no rain is forecast, if you wanted to come back Sunday.'

I was a little shocked by his lack of fibre. Seriously choked engines can't be cured quickly.

However, satisfaction was to come my way. I worked through Sunday while Marston walked with his hiking group up some nearby hills and Helena visited her family. She told me all about this as she was cooking our meal while I was preparing to tell her I had checked the spark plug to ensure the wire was connected firmly, not wobbling about. It *was* connected correctly, in fact, so I removed the spark plug and found it covered with corrosion. A simple scrubbing with a wire brush would restore it to working order. Did she have a wire brush? I asked her.

She stopped cooking and turned to face me. 'I've just told you my mother has pleurisy and you ask if I have a wire brush!'

'So sorry, I should have allowed a pause between your news and my enquiry.' But she wasn't pleased, and I'm sure my portion of mashed potato was smaller than originally intended. I enjoy my food, or rather hers. I don't cook myself, so getting properly fed is another bonus when I visit her. She says my shoulder bones stick out.

These hiccups aside, I was able to give her the better news that I had fixed both the wheel shafts. The best news of all I was saving until we were all three together and nearing that wonderful moment when I would mount the reconstructed machine and demonstrate its power from aloft.

On a warm and dry Thursday evening I phoned Helena and suggested popping round at tea-time. After a slice of cake and a couple of scones, we could nip over to the mower again, even if Marston wasn't in.

We had the tea, though scones weren't in evidence. I had to raid my car for a spare packet of Wagon Wheels.

'Shall we check on the mower now?'

Helena insisted on phoning Marston first. 'I never just *turn up!*' she said in a squealy tone. I thought I might mention that in bed later; something she might work upon (or against).

I'm sure Marston was delighted to see us again, and no-one had touched the mower parts since my last session. I had bought my own wire brush - a small diversion to the hardware store en route for Marston's - and so started on the spark plugs until they were immaculate. Next, it was to be the engine. I questioned Marston about its current noise. He described voice and timbre.

I told him, 'If it hunts and surges it may be experiencing something as simple as an airflow issue. If the air is blocked, and in particular, sporadically, the engine slows down. When the blockage clears, the engine suddenly revs up in response.' I demonstrated, which made him jump.

I laughed and held up the air filter, clogged with dirt and debris. 'Good news, Marston. I just need your washing-up bowl. Soapy water, please. I'll clean this out and check the vented gas cap. Then we'll have no sporadic air flow to trouble the engine. Its voice will be a pure liquid contralto.'

'I suppose I can buy a new washing-up bowl,' I heard Marston mutter to Helena whose eyes, I suddenly noticed, whizzed up to the ceiling at intervals. Poor love, it's not a pretty sight, so I'll advise her about avoiding doing that. Another topic for bedtime.

They returned. The washing-up bowl more than served its purpose, and when I handed it back, blacker than the air filter that spilled its guts into it, Marston said it didn't matter and put it with his recycling. Helena took it out again, insisting that the men wouldn't take severely soiled items. I waited for their exchanges to cease before holding up an air filter any lawn mower would be proud to display.

Now for the best bit. They were inside making coffee. I was reconstructing the scarlet shiny creature whose engine would now thrill them. While they'd idled their Sunday away, up hills and with family, I had solved the carburettor problem. Incorrect adjustment is apparently a common cause of poor engine idling. It results in hunting and surging. Fortunately, two screws allow you to adjust the carburettor. One screw controls the idle speed while the other adjusts the idle mixture. I'd succeeded in starting the mower and allowed it to run for five minutes before making these adjustments. It was then I identified the air flow issue, but Marston returned from the hills before I could complete my work.

Now all was fixed and by the time they came outside to check on me, the tractor stood together and ready. The sun was going down. I started the engine seductively. 'Well?'

'My word! Have you really fixed it? Will it work?'

'May I?' I placed a tentative foot on the nearside wheel.

'Please,' said Marston.

So I did. Climbing up, I sat for the first time on the shaped metal seat surveying my arena: a generous expanse of overgrown lawn. I looked down on them and felt bigger than a tractor. The engine sang with the joy of one whose lungs have been miraculously cured of consumption. As the sun set on the horizon, I mowed towards it, creating stripes in two shades of green for Marston to enjoy as far as his eyes could scan.

'What a picture,' yelled Helena. 'Your white t-shirt, the red tractor, and the sun going down on you. I've left you some sandwiches. I think I'll go home. Alone. I like my own space.'

The sound of the engine completely drowned her words. Marston told me what she'd said, some considerable time later. I couldn't understand why she'd gone without me.

Marston was so thrilled with my mowing. I'll be back when his grass grows, although he says he can't wait to do it himself. Helena lives with bumpy grassy areas all around her, so those must be treated with the kind of mowers you push. Never mind, I now have twenty-two in the barn to choose from.

I'm hoping to get friendly with the farmer when I meet him. He owns the three tractors, not so far in my touching distance. So, although Helena isn't totally in tune with me, I shall continue with the relationship. You have to persist with these things; they take time.

IN SMOKE

I found our special matchbox holder behind the old meat safe. It speaks of The Event that no-one dares mention.

Afterwards, I didn't see my father but as I open my keepsake box with its Festival of Britain badge, the very smell of him surges out: singed paper, charcoal, smoke. Inside the box lies our special matchbox holder. When I was little, Father painted it in crimson, emerald and gold on a black background. It was always the brightest thing in our kitchen. We three boys fought to be the one to hold it and strike the match.

It sat by the gas stove in those Before times and came into the garden with us on Sundays. That was when we had bonfires, exciting hours when we ran free and watched things light up, when we learned what burnt with a flash and what smouldered on and on, but never quite died.

Sophie didn't join in. She had a prefect's badge and breasts. I was sorry for her, left out of the fun. She said she was too grown-up to play with little brothers; anyway she couldn't escape from being Mother's helper.

Mother was always busy with her checklists and sanctions. When things got hairy we would run off, but Sophie had to stay and share the music. And Father had to listen to everything that had gone wrong, everything that had needed fixing all week.

On school-day mornings, Mother was less fearsome without

her hairpiece and maroon lips. She checked our satchels, our homework, our set books and told Father to get us into the car. As it turned the corner, we'd sing *Ten Green Bottles,* or if it had been a bitter breakfast, *Fire Down Below.*

After school, there was choir, cubs, homework for us, household repairs for Father. Sophie had cookery, and music practice. Her pile of homework, a tower of Pisa on her bedroom table as she peeped at Father from behind it, lifting her eyes far up under her eyebrows. He twitched the half of his mouth that didn't have nails between his teeth ready to bang things into place.

Monday nights were for planning and review. It was always a worry who had the worst school marks. They'd have the nastiest chores for the week. Mother was at her most severe and Father at his most vague. If he hadn't checked someone's spellings, we'd knock something off the table or kick each other so the blame got diverted. Father pursed his lips like a trumpeter who'd played a wrong note.

On Tuesdays, Mother took us to band. All of us played something, cornet, oboe, trombone. Father played the piano, but secretly, when Mother was out, because she didn't like him wasting time. His music rippled through the house like satin. I'd sit under the piano enjoying the vibrations and pop out to alert him when I heard Mother returning. He probably played when we were at band. Sophie wouldn't tell on him. She didn't go with us. The violin's only any good for an orchestra or duets. Violin and piano sound good together.

After band, we'd clatter back noisily so Father could look busy before Mother brought in the fish and chips. She'd call to him, 'Did you fix the leak in the cloakroom basin? You said you'd look at that sagging shelf…' and Father would say, 'All right, all right, I know.'

Mother was extra strict about homework on Wednesdays because we'd done none on Tuesdays. We sat round the dining table. Oilcloth covered the velvety one that was laid over the wood. We could press hard with our pencils and our marks didn't damage the surface.

'Your father will check your work, boys.'

Father peered over my shoulder, 'This looks all right to me.'

'But look at his scrawly writing. You can't let him get away with that. It's slapdash, worse than his brother's, although he's nearly two years older.'

I'd feel a nudge. My next brother would hide his grin and I'd kick him under the table.

My smallest brother groaned and sighed and put down his pencil.

Mother tutted. 'He doesn't understand what to do. You'll have to explain,' and my father did.

My brother got muddled and cried, curling away from Mother's cross voice, 'Oh, let him sort it out for himself.' But while she wasn't looking, Father did it for him, winked at us all, and closed the book.

After homework, Mother rubbed flat hands together as if erasing all our mistakes. Then she'd turn to Father. 'You still haven't seen to that shelf. One day it will collapse and then where shall we be?'

Father said, 'Well I can't do it NOW. I'd better check upstairs.' He'd help Sophie in her room and sometimes he was gone a long time. Afterwards, he'd take his briefcase and do his office work in the study, all hunched up and private.

Thursday was bath night. Mother took the matchbox and lit the big white heater over the bath through its little front hole. A flame showed, glimmering. 'You must none of you ever try to turn the heat on. Gas without flame is very dangerous.' The matchbox in its brilliant holder waited on the Lloyd Loom basket where it wouldn't get wet.

Mother went out while we undressed because she didn't want to see our ugly bits. We peered at the little flame through its hole, nudging each other and saying, '*Sunday.*' When the hot tap turned on, the little flame burst into life, a minor explosion, so thrilling it made us laugh, Sundays in our minds. Sundays: no school, no chores, no homework and the promise of fireworks. We dared each other to put our hands on the water heater to feel the whirrs and pops of the fire hidden under the white metal cover. Truly hot water spurted out of the tap. All other times we washed in cold water, even in January, because we were British. We relished Thursday's bath nights, getting into hot water.

When we were washed and dried and huddled into our towels, we opened the bathroom door and there was Mother, almost smiling. She liked us when we were newly clean.

Normally we walked home after school with Mother, but Father brought us home on Friday afternoons because we had football, he ended work early and it was Sophie and Mother's cooking day. As the front door opened, wonderful baking smells surged towards us but there was no room in the steamy kitchen for noisy boys. We'd hover in the passage breathing in the promise of pastry and cake before sloping off to do our homework.

Eventually, Sophie laid the table and we'd be called for tea. There'd be cheese fingers, crumpets, queen cakes, Victoria sponge and trifle.

When Father finished the jobs Mother had set him, he slid onto his chair with a small grin to us. He looked glumly at the near-empty serving plates with their crumby doilies, but we'd saved him a piece of tart and a crumpet, and there was always lots of Victoria sponge left over because Mother never spread enough jam in the middle. Sophie always hid extra cakes in her napkin covered by her apron. We never told on her. She might have needed more cakes to fill her breasts, or perhaps they were secret treats for Father when he helped her with her homework.

If Father looked for another slice of cake, Mother would say, 'About that sagging shelf under the stairs ...'

Once I said, 'He'll need to be a contortionist,' and everyone giggled, except Mother. The shelf was right at the back where the cupboard sloped down low. It was a good place to hide in. Father caught Mother's gleaming eye. 'I'm just getting round to that job, but it's tricky.' He disappeared into the dark at the back of the house.

On Saturdays, we stayed in bed late. Then we had toast and dripping and competed over who could eat most. When Father got back with the shopping, he ate the cold leavings. Meanwhile, we put the shopping away. We liked seeing his finds. Mother would say, 'Why did you waste money on jam?' or 'The children shouldn't have so many biscuits,' or 'You know I don't like kidneys.'

We'd get busy with cutting out or puzzles or making models on the kitchen table. Mother said, 'I'm fed up with this clutter,' so we took our ugly bits into our bedroom and played there. We passed Sophie at her mirror trying out make-up. She raised blackened eyebrows at us. We were boys and messy people, but we wouldn't tell on her.

We made cardboard cannons and Eiffel Towers, paper aeroplanes and folded birds, then threw away the cuttings and origami failures, choking with laughter at the overflowing waste baskets. 'Look at mine!' 'Mine's fuller.' 'No, no, look at mine!'

While we were constructing, cutting, folding and pasting, Mother and Father were busy downstairs with letters, bills and paper work, notes to remind them about doing other things, problems to discuss. Saturday was a really busy day for them.

If we went downstairs, we might be sent to play Monopoly in the front room without quarrelling. That used to take us nearly all day.

In the afternoon, Father went on mending things, writing things, paying things. He tried to get round to the sagging shelf, but other things got in the way. 'I'll just put these hooks up in the kitchen, first.' His wireless utility set lurked in a dark corner where it reported exciting sport. He took up his saw and looked at the wall for a long time. He measured up carefully. One of us might hold the nails or the pencil while Father held up a rule.

Mother said, 'It's no good just looking at it!' He said, 'It's sensible to plan ahead,' but she went on talking, her voice drowning the football scores. Behind her back, Sophie put her head round the door, her lips bright red, to see if she could get away with it. Father gave her a quick wink, secretly, as he listened to Mother and said 'Yes', his head leant towards the wireless.

There could be trouble.

But Sundays was bonfire day and Father was the bonfire king. He collected the cuttings from the hedge or bushes and set light to the products of the week. If there was really nothing to burn – no dried leaves, branches or cuttings – if there had been nothing to mow short, cut back, cut down, trim, shape or snip, Father sent us indoors to bring back waste paper, letters, postcards, bills, jigsaws with missing pieces, drawings, paintings, cardboard models, cut-outs and throw-outs, and he would burn those.

In summer our bonfires were small, but in autumn they spiralled into the air, legitimate at last. The dying leaves lay round in lumps, swept up by one of us. The air smelt of pine before the bonfire was lit, charcoal later.

We ran round like maniacs sniffing in the bonfire smell. Although Sophie's face was pressed to her window, she hardly noticed us. She was watching Father's antics. With Mother out of view, he leapt like a dancer, his uplifted hand scattering a mound of dry leaves to make a halo round his head. Sophie sat back with a little smile. Father looked up at her window and he was smiling too.

Once the flames took hold, his face screwed up against the smoke, his body ducked down against the heat. He poked hard to get the fire higher. Then he threw on his fodder and bent low to blow embers into flames. We didn't like to intrude upon the urgency of it. There was no way of talking to him without entering the coughing and spluttering zone. We couldn't get near him without being spattered with black and grey flak.

Father shored up the pyre, poking and prodding with deep concentration while we watched admiringly. Occasionally he turned and looked at us with a faraway smile. But he never taught us how to make a bonfire. Indoors, afterwards, we elbowed each other to sit close enough to breathe in his charcoal smell, swallow it deep. We grew up believing bonfires were complex pieces of artwork - Father's creation.

There were very few Sundays without a bonfire. In the wet and snow, Father lit bonfires in the metal box at the back of the garden. At the end of the spluttering and flaming, escaped papers billowed away with their singed information. The bonfire was just a dirty mess hateful against the shining paths and untouched snow in the rest of the garden. We slouched indoors, deflated.

Father's green rubbery cape encompassed him so completely

that only the feet of his wellingtons arrived at the back door, muddy and wet. The cape went on a hook in the lean-to, then he sat on the step, pulling off his sodden wellies like a criminal. Mother watched from the gleaming kitchen floor, hands on her hips, before he trespassed in his socks.

Sophie's violin music floated down the stairs. 'We should sell that violin,' said Mother. 'She's not getting any better.' She glared at Father. 'She should have learned the French horn. I *told* you.'

The last time I saw Father, he was lying on his front, legs splayed out across the hall. I thought he was dead, but he was only fixing the sagging shelf under the stairs. The violin sang from Sophie's room and I knew my cornet would never sound as sweetly.

We went off to band practice and when we got back the house was dark. Mother put the lights on and called 'Sophie!', but no-one answered.

I wanted to avoid the trouble. I held on to both my brothers and told Mother, 'See? Father's fixed the sagging shelf.' She opened the cupboard under the stairs and found the shelf as firm as a church. She called to Father, then to Sophie again. The silent house echoed with her voice.

She rushed up to her room, then Sophie's. We heard her throw open cupboards, drawers, and after some minutes, her own bedroom door slammed. My middle brother goggle-eyed me and I didn't know what to do. From Mother's closed room, coughing sounds trickled down the stairs. My little brother put his thumb in his mouth.

We crept into the kitchen and ate our fish and chips out of the paper. Mother's went cold, the paper soggy and soiled under her battered fish. We looked at her greasy chips, then at each other. I gave a nod, and we went quickly to bed.

In the morning, we sidled downstairs to the empty kitchen. 'Where is she?' my next brother whispered. Without the news rumbling in the background it was clear I should take charge. I put out the cereal bowls, the cups, milk and spoons. I tied my little brother's shoe-laces.

Then Mother came down. Her hairpiece was crooked, her lips colourless.

Over the Rice Krispies packet I scowled at the other two, like a warning.

It didn't stop my youngest brother. 'Where's Father? Isn't he coming back?'

Mother shook her head. 'No. Nor is your sister. So you needn't say any more about either of them.'

My other brother blurted, 'She'll be late for school.' That was a dreadful sin.

Mother swallowed and muttered. 'No more school for her.'

'But she's a *prefect*!' My elbow in his side shut him up at last.

She looked at me, perhaps she'd forgotten my name. 'You're the oldest now. You'll have to fix things. Tonight I'll sort out - her - room and you can have it.'

My next brother scowled and opened his mouth to say *It's not fair* but she was going on. 'You must take the others to school and you'll just have to learn how to do jobs.'

I pulled on my jacket and told the others to come on. Middle brother and I held on to the little one to get him out of the house. He pulled our hands. 'I want to see Father.' We shushed him and hurried him off to school. It was a long walk.

Middle brother kicked at stray stones. 'Sophie's gone. Not fair. Why didn't he take me?'

Little brother said, 'You aren't a prefect.'

I didn't say, 'And you haven't got breasts.'

* * *

We didn't go to band after Father left.

'Look what happens if we leave the house on a regular basis,' said Mother. We didn't mention The Event ever again. We knew better.

We don't need a meat safe anymore. We have a refrigerator. Mother modernised. We don't need matches, the cooker is electric and there's bar heaters. The water heats by electricity, you just press a switch. The radio has long wave as well as medium and short. It's beige and shiny and small enough to pick up and carry into any room you want. On the news this morning we heard, "You've never had it so good."

So there's no use for a matchbox holder, but before Mother threw it away, I rescued it. I think Father left its brightness in a safe place for one of us to find, so we'd think about bonfires after he'd gone. I want to hold onto it, smell it and remember the Before times. I've put it in my private keepsake box with the *Men Only* magazine I found in the shed, and my National Savings book.

Although that sagging shelf is still holding up, Mother finds me a list of jobs every evening. My brothers are grumpy so I have to fix them too or Mother will say she can't cope. She's stopped checking our homework. We've stopped making models. 'You boys must face Real Life,' Mother said. 'I have to.'

We've practised our music in the evenings all year, so now we play well enough for band on Saturdays, and Sundays are just for outside jobs. Provided we get everything done, I'm allowed to play the piano. Someone has to. When my fingers make the music come, my secret thoughts float out and in the faint distance I hear duets - piano and violin.

Before Father went away, Sundays were always for bonfires and now they're gone; no flare-ups, no flickering flames, not even a smouldering ember. When I look from my bedroom window where Sophie once knelt, there's not a leap or a sparkle to see. Sophie's got them. Father took Sophie and left us the matchbox holder. He took our fire and just left smoke.

THE RETURN 1919

You didn't believe it, did you? When the white cliffs of Dover rose like ghost sheets, figments of your imagination. When the demob said 'Here's your travel pass,' it hardly made sense. They let you go, unfettered.

In a dream, your feet took you to Victoria station, the old platform, crowded, people in civvies around you staring at the side of your face, your hand, one saying 'Come on, Soldier. Watch out, go easy. I'll help you on board.'

Now sitting on a seat, not standing, peering from the train windows thick with dirt, your eyes so sore. You didn't believe it when the train spurted along that familiar route. Here are the same signboards, tattered ads for Syrup of Figs, Bovril, same filthy factory buildings, although some things different, gaps between them, gaping house fronts, rubble.

It's raining a bit. This *is* England. Blighty. Blimey, mate, you're released, you've survived the camp, that long march out of it, not like the others. But you had to make it. Doreen waiting for you. Three years. And now you're going home. Stop laughing, stop crying, they're looking at you. People. Brits.

Look, the train's coming into that station, yours. You see the school first, its bell tower, a dreaded sight once but wonderful now. That ugly little brick building with the lavs in the playground, always a desperate run away. Your mates use to tease you about your chubby red cheeks. Ha! And you had good hands in those days with all your fingers, all your nails. You'd be yawking as loud as the others, whinging about school—all you had to rant about, then.

Surely, you never used to be able to see the school from the station; the factory chimneys were in the way? But, see, they're gone. Several of the works too. Just a pile of rubble. You're used to that, where you've been. Brick rubble, tons of rubble. That's what the Turks made you do, heave rubble onto trucks. Heave it until you were dropping from exhaustion, too spent to grieve about those who had dropped already, you were too creased by your hunger. But that's all over now, isn't it? Rescued, freed, demob. Sixpence for your greatcoat, new clothes three sizes smaller than you used to take.

She might not recognize you, Doreen. Even though she'll have been waiting by the gate every night for the last few years, wondering where you are. Your woman, your little wife. Lovely girl, she's been the one who kept you going through the misery, the indignity; her image your one weapon against the brutal guards, shit-holes.

Why think of all that now? This is your station. Go on, stumble out. You're standing on the platform. You know exactly where to go. Move forward! Some of it's familiar. That poster's gone, the Gibson girl with her white teeth, the toothpaste you yearned for these last years almost as much as the girl, your girl, that smile.

Up this road, turn left. That's the same, the whole terrace standing. Someone at a gate staring. You turn your bad side away, walk down that parallel road, Victory Road. Nice it's still called that! All still standing, too. No, a gap at the end where the newsagents used to be. You liked him, that old man, always a quip with your *Men Only* mag. Wonder if he copped it, standing inside his doorway?

Turn right. Right again where the road curves. It's getting closer, your road. There's the Congregational church, a poster saying *Jesus loves You.* He didn't seem to, the last few years. You went off him, big time. See that notice? They've changed the time for Sunday School, always used to be eleven o'clock, didn't it? You used to save the stickers, stamps, really, with Jesus stories on them; put them in the notebook Mum gave you, tearing out her shopping lists first. That notebook's gone, Mum's gone, although she tried to get to a shelter. Learned about all that just before you got captured, one thing after another, let's not speak about it. Enemy kept you busy enough you didn't think. Don't think now.

There it is. Your road, the bottom end. Your stomach's jumping. It's because it doesn't feel real, coming home. There'll be some torture waiting, heavy labour, teeth pulling, something. Guards round the corner, behind that hut. Watch out!

Oh! There's the butcher's shop, plaster meat in the window but you can *smell* meat as you pass. You had meat this last week, in that hut near the demob. Made you ill after; so long since you had a round meal, square meal, any meal. Slops, rice, that's been your lot for - what two years, three, more? Lost count. Lost being able to count.

If that shop was open, you could buy nice chops for her supper like you did before the war. Chops! You can't get chops! She'll have to tell you what you can get, and where you go and queue. You don't know. She'll put you in the picture so you can pull your weight while you're "taking it easy for a while" until it's time to line up at the labour exchange, get a job, a civvy job. Some job, somehow.

Look at your legs, left and righting. They're doing the unbelievable, walking down your own road, your kitbag tapping your back, packed up troubles in it, not much else. You could only save her a bar of chocolate. Hardly go shopping where you were! Shopping! Ha ha. Ha, ha, ha! Stop it. Stop laughing, you're making a spectacle of yourself. Someone will see you.

Into your road. Look around. Can't see anyone you know. Kids gawping at your flapping trouser legs, their own knees scabby with playing marbles. One eyeballs your face, goes weird and hides behind a tree. One's got a bike of sorts, no brakes, he'll come a cropper one of these days. He wouldn't be Kenny Nobbins, would he? It's years since you saw the little blighter. No, Kenny will be a grown lad now. Look inside number twelve as you pass, door's open. Some old girl in a pinny, coming up the hall with her washload. No sign of a Kenny.

Getting nearer. When you get over this hilly bit you'll see your house, your own place. Bend over, breathe hard. Belly hurts from wanting to see it so long.

Can't see it yet, come on, come on. Cripes, you're jumpy. She might be wearing that blue dress, that one she used to wear at the Locarno. The Locarno where she gave you a navy spot tie and a kiss and you said you'd paint the hall wall for her Dad. And soon after, you were off, brave soldier, seeing her tears, imagining her proud expression all the way to the port. That face, that body, yours, been watching for you all these years, never knowing what you were going through. Now you'll tell her. She'll cry again. Don't say, then. Don't tell. It's not for her ears. Not for anyone's, likely.

Turn at the bend. Number eighteen, twenty's there. All the twenties are there, except for twenty-nine, grass where there used to be a porch. Now there's a front door to nothing. The thirties have copped it, some of them. Now the forties. Thank God yours missed it. Didn't it? Check. Breathe. All right and dandy all the way to the top end of the road - but the numbers have stopped.

Are we there? You can't work out what number this one would be, so—walk on. Next one? No. Jesus! Which house is yours? They all look the same, sod it. Stupid, stupid. You must know your own house. Black gate. But they've all got black gates.

You're panicking, aren't you? Is this one yours? No. Yes. No. Calm down. Ask someone. Ask.

'Scuse me mate, who lives here, do you know? Was this number forty-eight? Is it? Was it?'

'Slow down, soldier, steady on. It is forty-eight. You're okay, take it easy. The Bowes live here. Right?'

'*Bowes*. Right.' Wrong, wrong.

Bloke walks on. She must have taken lodgers to make ends meet. The Bowes. You know no Bowes. You no-no-bowes! Stop laughing, she'll think you're crazy. If you ever get yourself down the path.

You don't have your key anymore, your anything. Don't have

the key of the door, never been twenty-one before, never will be. That's not funny. No key. So knock. Knock and see. Look at that fancy brass thing - new. A lion face on it! Give it a bang. That's right. Sweaty hands, slip on the knocker. Bang, bang.

Footsteps. You might faint. Pass out. Ha ha, jokey joke. You passed out long ago.

Step back, the door's opening. Open your eyes. It's her face! For real! Her lovely face. It doesn't smile. The mouth opens, the face pales. She's gawping something awful. She says something. It isn't "Darling! You're back!" It's 'O-oh' and 'Oh my God, is it…?' and her eyes are like moons.

'Oh, Raaaaay.' Her hands are up to her mouth like she's holding it onto her face. She's very white. Stand there, keep on standing there looking at her, your dream. Wait for the tears, the arms to come out to you. Give her a moment, it's a shock, you can see. It's been a long, long time. Did you say that? No, your words haven't started yet.

Behind her, you can see right down the hall, your hall. The cream gloss on the lower part where the criss-cross pattern defeated your brush, beast it was when you painted it, day before you left, a lifetime ago. She's left the door of the parlour open. The table's laid. Two places. Some slippers, men's slippers, grey-trousered knees, you can't see the rest. You've never had slippers like that; never had slippers – have you?

You want to say, 'I'm back, Doreen darling. I'm back,' take her in your arms, at last, at last. The words won't come.

She still hasn't stretched out her hands, touched you. Those places she used to know must look so different now, some of them gone altogether. You don't dare touch her. Not with these hands.

She's reeling back. She lifts her shoulders, the tops of her arms like it's too much for her to say or do anything. Then she does. She wrings her hands. 'Oh, Ray. What have they done to you?'

It doesn't matter now, she'll make it better. So your throat lets you say it. 'Kiss me, darling wife. See, I got back home.'

She startles, 'No,' she says. One hand goes out, palm down. 'Remember, Ray?' Her head moves from side to side. 'We finished when you joined up. I told you not to. You would go, and now look at you.' She cries. You watch her tears. This time they're because you've returned, not because you're leaving.

I shake my head, flies in it or something. 'I married you, lived here, painted that wall.' I poke out my arm, point. I shouldn't have let her see that hand.

She jerks back, eyes widen. She shakes her head, hair all over the place, getting wet with tears. 'You painted it for Dad, long before we dated. And Dad's dead, too.' She turns towards the parlour, their parlour.

A man comes out. 'What's going on, Doreen?'

'This is Ray. He's back from …'

'P.O.W.,' you mutter. 'Kut. Middle East.'

'Jeeze, mate. They made a mess of you. Lived near here, did you?'

Did I? Didn't I live here, with Doreen? Didn't I woo her, marry her?

She says, 'Look at him, his poor hands. I should've been told.' She sobs, leans back on the man. He comforts her.

'She's real upset. Take it easy now, mate. Rest up. You've earned it. Tomorrow, come up the Kings Arms. I'll buy you a drink. The others will too.'

She lets a sob gush out. He comes up behind her, puts his unmarked hands, thick fingers, wide nails, either side of her waist.

You can't bear it. You can't. Words come out of your dried up mouth, spittle forms at the cracks. 'What are you doing here?'

'What? I live here.'

'No.'

She wails. 'I don't know what to do, Len. His brain's gone. We went out twice, he thinks he lives here.'

Only twice? You'd been staring at her for weeks, like the war wouldn't come; she in the shop window, you on your delivery bike. You know this house, this hall. You remember painting it. Didn't you carry her into it after taking her down the aisle?

'Oh, Ra-ay …' Too much crying stops her saying any more. She doesn't need to. He cuddles her, looks at you, frowning.

'Look, mate. Ray. You're muddled. War's been a bad deal for

you. Get yourself sorted, now. We'll look out for you, down the Kings. All right for cigs, money?'

You nod. Cigs, money, that's what you've got. Ration book's in your pocket. Time to move off.

You know what you have to do. Qu-ick march! Left, right, left. Through the black gate.

For-ward! Right turn. Re-turn!

Where?

THE PRICE OF PRESENCE

Presence they call it. It's rather like that 'something' they search for in performers. Star quality.

Barclay had it, even at eighty-two. One glance at him and you felt you were with a celebrity, although he said he'd never been well-known. Standing, he was nearly at my eye level and I'm over six foot. His back was still straight though he needed sticks. His full head of hair stood out amongst the baldies in the residence. Barclay had far more than me. Unfair!

I'm not being disrespectful when I call him Barclay; it's his Christian name. You can't use "Mr Wordesley", or "Mr Aruba" or whatever when you're sitting them on the loo. Formal at one end and exceedingly intimate at the other: it wouldn't work.

And the patients don't call me *Mr* either. That would be nice, but I can't expect it. My previous job at A and E brought me more respect. The agency doesn't care about respect. They said I was lucky to be employed at all after the bit of bother at the hospital. They weren't eager to engage me again, just shrugged and suggested Care work was available. Truth is, they had to employ me, they're so short of Care people, particularly male workers. There have been complaints from male oldies because it's humiliating for their personal needs to be met by a woman, especially as it may be a different one each time. That's another advantage about male carers: we don't phone in to cancel because of sick children or school holidays.

I've cornered rather a nice little routine between retirement residences, rarely having to see to the women, thank the Lord.

Shame not to be doing Barclay anymore. He was the easiest of my patients. Although I'm "only" a Care Support Worker, I like to call them *patients* because they certainly have to be, the time they have to wait for my visits. I won't be rushed to keep to the obligatory twenty minute slots. It's fine for them in the office. They don't see how much we have to do at each call.

I tell my gentlemen, 'I'd rather be late, and do you properly, is that all right?' They always nod because they don't want to be the one who's short-changed, especially in the bathroom department. If I happen to mention the loss of pay the extra time I've spent with them has cost me, they usually make it up or I get little presents. Sometimes it'll be antiques, "just something I won't need anymore. Have to de-clutter when you're my age." That's what they say. It's nice when Acme Antiques expresses an interest in my pieces. It would be a shame not to sell them when the shop's so keen to display them.

There was often a documentary on the radio when I called on Barclay. Such an educated man. However late I was, he never complained, never listed all his latest symptoms. Quite a refreshing change. It showed how highly he valued me. There are other carers, but I'm known as the one who really cares.

I'd noticed all the other residents in his block of flats respected Barclay, "A good, god-fearing man." "Such a Christian fellow." That's what they thought about him.

One day I said, 'Barclay, the others all think of you as a keen Christian but you haven't got the crosses and religious bits and bobs they have.'

'No, and I don't go to church, either.'

I had to be careful how to answer that. You never know if a patient practices another religion. You might say the wrong cultural thing.

Barclay was a book-lover. He dusted them all himself but I often took a good look. There weren't any bibles or prayer books amongst them. Surprising, really, for someone described as "God-fearing". I couldn't help asking, 'When did you stop going to church then, Barclay?'

'As soon as I was old enough to have any say. Eighteen in those days! Just think, all those Sundays sentenced to a hard pew listening to words I didn't believe, singing hymns to someone who, as far as I'm concerned, doesn't exist.'

'But your upbringing. Weren't your parents keen church-goers?'

'Ah, yes indeed. Extremely keen. Wisely, I held my counsel.'

He talked like that, a professor-type, Barclay was. I think he actually was a professor. His subject was *Anthropology*. He taught me how to pronounce the word when he explained what it meant. On his high shelf stood little heads, black with curly hair strands. If they'd once been real, and bigger, I didn't ask. I wouldn't ever touch them.

While I cleaned out his fridge and prepared his tea, I got him to tell me why he wasn't a believer like his parents.

He smirked and leant back in his recliner. 'I was still in the infants' school when an accidental encounter showed me not all adults hung together like neatly bagged coats on a dry cleaners' rail.'

'Barclay, the way you put things. You do make me laugh. Go on.'

'A well-brought-up, respectful child, I was class monitor and trusted to take messages. Coming round the bend of the staff corridor with my teacher's note, I found Mr Woodley (Class Six) and Mr Briggs (Class Five) chuckling. That was shock enough - that adults, *teachers* - joked. But worse! I followed their joint gaze out of the window. Trundling across the playground was Mrs Auberon in her bath chair. She taught Religious Instruction as well as Singing. They were laughing at *her*!

'Until then, I'd seen teachers as a solid flank of chequered trouser and flannel skirt ranged against a rabble of rumpled socks and out-hanging vests, kicked shins, bruised knees, whispers, giggles and stray gleeful shouts.'

'Ho! Yes, that about sums kids up.'

'Yet the teachers' laughter showed me the flank was not solid after all! It had chinks.

'All those months of my school life so far, I had imagined Mrs Auberon to be a piteous beast whose vicious temper, mean pinching, slapping and ruler-snapping were borne of great pain, injury, illness or close sight of death. She taught us about Jesus and led our prayers, so she must be closest to God. In her fiercest mode, she taught us the Lord's Prayer. She said it was our word to God that we would always be honest. We must recite the prayer, keep our eyes shut, and believe in Him.

'But here were Mr Briggs and Mr Woodley with their brown sports jackets, big heads and scratchy-looking chins, men who wrote squiggles on the blackboard that no-one understood but everyone copied down, laughing aloud and *at* a righteous person —Mrs Auberon, as she trundled out of the school gate in her black carriage, the wheels dutifully turned by Little Benny Blunkett. Poor Benny, social isolate, grubby, often dunced in the corner by Mrs Auberon for such long periods that he wet his already stinky shorts. This prize victim was pushing Mrs Auberon's carriage along the playground and through the gates to The Outside.

'I heard Mr Biggs snort, "She's a darn sight more capable of walking out of the gates than that poor little chap!"

'They laughed again, and turned to sign my teacher's docket. They only seemed to see the note, ignoring me as if I was deaf and blind.

'Their laughter seemed a sacrilege to me. If Mrs Auberon could walk out of the school unaided, then she was a fraud. She had not been honest about needing someone to wheel her around. She had cheated God. She was not someone to be sorry for or remember in our night prayers.

'That made me alert to other adult claims to godliness. The vicar came to give a school assembly wearing the cassock I'd always thought he'd been born in, like an angel. He stood on the stage preaching about being kind to others. I already knew one teacher who wasn't. When he'd finished his sermon and led the prayers, he approached the stage steps, lifting his cassock a little. I spotted ordinary trouser bottoms, black, just like my father's. I realised then the vicar was just an ordinary man dressed up!

'So how could I grow up a believer? Disillusioned by Mrs Auberon's fraud and the vicar's disguise, I digested my new knowledge. It was like a secret power—I had unmasked them without them realising. I could recite the Lord's Prayer off by heart, but now I only muttered it while keeping my eyes open and my mind closed.

'In the further years of church going, I blocked out prayers and sermons by silently rehearsing my times tables and later, Latin declensions. When I left home, I renounced every last vestige of religion, vowing only to honour honesty.'

'That was a long time to keep your thoughts to yourself, Barclay!'

'Yes indeed. As I've mentioned, it was best to remain silent on the subject of God. The various religious artefacts given me as presents by my parents and other church members were an accumulation of trash, in my eyes. It was hard, comparing my godly presents with school friends' boxes of chocolates or the latest album. It has been my delight to off-load that religious claptrap to dear people here who value such things.'

Barclay's disclosure was an eye opener to me. So that's why they all respected the person they assumed was religious! 'You gave the crosses and things away as presents?'

'People are always so pleased, and the price of presents is abysmal, isn't it? My income is sadly inadequate, these days.' He paused, his head turning towards the iridescent glass bowl where he kept pound coins. He'd already told me the Loetz Art Nouveau bowl was his one precious possession. I was resigned to disappointment: I wouldn't be having that as "a little thank you".

Barclay stood up and faced me, eye to eye. 'So my heart and mind remained loyal to the concept of honesty. I was going to give you my leather-bound prayer-book for Christmas, an extravagant present, but deserved by *The One who Cares*. It was when I saw you helping yourself to my savings I decided you might prefer to keep those pound coins instead. They certainly add up, don't they? And I came to the conclusion you weren't a church-goer.'

My mobile phone was ringing, I'm sure it was. 'Sorry, Barclay. Someone needs me urgently. Must rush. Some people have no patience.'

MAKING IT

Ma said to Dawnie, 'Well, in that case, I suppose I shall have to meet him.'

Her daughter led her the few streets away and up some steps to a cracked door. It opened some minutes after Dawnie's knock. They waited on the step, looking up.

She saw his feet first. His toe-nails long and curved, jagged, uncut, one of them gnarled. Nasty, probably, in kickboxing. Above the nails, hairy feet, pale jeans without hems hanging sloppily on long thighs. A jack-knife body and a face somewhere. For a seventeen-year-old, he hadn't much hair. Limp, futile strands dangled on a slack neck.

Ma attempted a smile. 'Hi.'

The lips parted around a soggy fag. 'Uh. Got ya.'

So this was Gary.

They followed him into the shared hallway past parts of a motorbike, a greasy anorak and a large broken carton full of discarded beer cans and CDs. There were four blokes living here. Growling came from a room at the back.

Gary opened a door and tossed a hand towards a doggy sofa. He didn't say 'Sit' but he meant it. Deep lines bracketed the tomb of his mouth. He yawned, then motioned towards some empty but stained mugs, 'Dyerwanter drink?'

Ma smiled a 'No thanks,' and looked into his eyes. They watered - a drinker's emotional eyes. One wandered.

Did he know what she was thinking, because he said, 'I tell people to look at me left eye. Me right's nearly blind,' neatly wronging her at a swipe. Gary pulled his lips sideways into a smile.

Ma thought of Action Man - plastic body, gripping hands, eagle eyes. Pull the lever to move his mouth.

Oh watch out, Dawnie, watch out.

When Dawn took Ma over his, she was glad it was Gary who answered and not one of the others. They'd be high by now, and well past caring about their manners. She needed Ma to approve of Gary.

But she needn't have worried. Gary looked so spruced up. Bless him, he'd showered and put on all clean stuff just as she'd begged him to when she'd said, 'If we're going to make it, I'll have to bring Ma to meet you.'

Gary showed Dawn and Ma where to sit. Amazing - there was no gear on the sofa! He'd even got Demon shut away to muffle his throaty growl and hyena wail.

'Would you like a drink?' Gary said, ever so nicely.

Course Ma wouldn't, because of the dirty mugs, but she would've liked his manners.

There wasn't a thing Ma could disapprove of. No splits in his jeans. No words on the T-shirt. He even wore a belt. Bit of a buckle on it, but still.

The things Gary had done for Dawn! Even cut off his hair last week. She'd been surprised how small his head was, after. He had his eighteenth coming up. Did you stop growing then?

Although he'd got dressed in time for Ma, Gary hadn't quite got around to his trainers but his dear feet glowed. She wanted to kiss the blue veins along the arch of his foot, the hairs on his big toes, and watch his kneecaps bend and straighten, click, crack, like plastic over metal joints, as he climbed upstairs.

Ma liked to see people tidy in clean clothes with short hair, talking nice. And it was all right! Gary was trying real hard. He even tried to make it easy for Ma, explaining about his poor eye. It was so sad, and his eyes watered when he said about it. She wanted to grab him and make it better, but really only a stiff drink would.

All right for some, looking at the world and seeing all of it! Gary could only see the sinister side, and it was down to her, Dawn, to describe the right side to him. He didn't always want to know. Bless him.

Ma was fed up of this school thing. All the phone calls, "We haven't see Dawn today". It was so difficult to get her daughter to go. If Dawnie didn't like school, what was *she* supposed to do about it?

It wasn't like Dawnie not to want her breakfast egg. Come to think of it, she had been looking a bit off-colour for a while. She wasn't too old to be taken to the doctor for a check, or the duty nurse if there were no appointments for weeks. Probably she needed vitamins or something.

Poor Dawnie was facing school exams soon. They weren't easy. She wanted to help, but when she'd peeped in the books, the work looked so hard. It was all stuff she hadn't done at school herself. Even if she'd just helped with the spelling, Dawnie's awful scrawl, and the long empty parts of the page left so little to work on. And Dawn wasn't keen on writing, so any attempts at improvement would be such an uphill task you'd slither back down—crash.

In the end, Ma let Dawnie stay at home some days. She'd been so tired, poor love. Vitamins might help.

Ma raked around in the back of the kitchen cabinet. It wobbled. It would be nice if she had a man around to fix that sort of thing. Still... bit late now. She hadn't had a bloke since Den, and he was a pain in the arse, though she missed him.

She found the vitamins. They were a bit old, gone over their date by a year, but they smelled all right. 'Dawnie, I want you to take a couple of these. Perk you up; you look pale.'

'Aw, leave off, Ma.'

'I'm going to take you up the health centre for a checkup but until we get an appointment, take these. You need them.'

'I need a fag and I'm having one, right?'

Ma couldn't stop to argue. If she wasn't on the veg. counter by 8.45 a.m. then Bernice would be, and Ma would have to go on shelves. Everyone hated shelf-stacking, and you had to answer those stupid questions: "Can you tell me where the tartare sauce is, please?" (by the effing sauces, of course). "You Rem," Dawnie would have added. But Ma was careful with her name-calling because it had been a near thing whether Dawn got put in the remedial class.

As she left for work, Ma saw Dawnie through the kitchen window, blue fluffy slippers up on the table, fag in her mouth. Perhaps she'd have washed-up by the time Ma got home. More likely, Dawnie'd be off up to Gary's as soon as she'd got dressed. Perhaps he'd walk her to school for late registration. No, not likely. What they did after Gary had signed on was anyone's guess. Fifteen, Dawnie was. What chance was there of getting her to listen to a mother?

~

God! At last Ma'd sodded off! To that dreary supermarket, rushing off dead early just to work on the veg. instead of the shelves. Why the fuck would anyone want to work all day when she'd get as much money on benefit: single parent, bad leg, that counted. On benefits, she wouldn't have to get up at all. Dawn wouldn't have been up, either, if she didn't feel queasier lying down. It wasn't fair. Like having a hangover without the booze. Still, this thing had been her idea. If she was going to get her own place with Gary, she had to start early.

Dawn hadn't actually told Ma yet. Since she'd taken Ma round Gary's, she'd been waiting for Ma to say something nice like, "You two make a lovely couple," or hear her tell the neighbours,

"My daughter's nice young man..." which would've made it easier. But Ma didn't say anything to the neighbours. She hadn't said anything to Dawn, really. Perhaps she wasn't that pleased about Gary. And Dawn needed Ma to be pleased or who else would put him up? Underage, she couldn't move out, and anyway Gary's mates wouldn't let her kip at his.

She stubbed out her cigarette on Ma's plate and looked at the washing-up. Sometimes Ma got in a mood if it was still there when she got back after work. There weren't that many dishes so it wouldn't take Ma long to do them herself but it wasn't worth a row, given Dawn might have to let on before long. Unless she just waited until Ma noticed the bump. She might keep things secret for a while, serve Ma right.

She looked at her white mobile. That fat bloke, "Dad", had passed it on to her. It only had credit sometimes but she could use the display. It wasn't time to phone Gary, not for several hours. No point. He wouldn't answer until 11.30 at the earliest. She might as well be in bed. Should she go back to bed now? Or watch Jeremy Kyle and the losers ranting on? She could do with a laugh.

Gary was a night bird. Dawn was pleased about that. When they lived together, they'd get up after mornings were over. That would be great. She didn't want some geek with a shirt and tie, off to some office at eight a fucking morning. She wanted to live!

She told Gary to meet her in the park so they could be a couple in public. It was a laugh because three months in, and she still hadn't told him, but she would today. They hadn't seen each other for a week because Gary's Dad had come down from the Wirral and they were up the greyhound track all the time. Now he'd gone back, thank God.

Gary had got up this morning for his appointment. He'd had his disability certificate updated by the doctor. He was fit for some work. That might be a drag.

'You going to get work, then, Gary?'

He drew himself up almost straight and put a hand on her head, manly like.

'I can work, find a job. Just not what the Job Centre's got.' He pulled out some papers from his hoodie. 'Here. You gotta help me fill in these to say what jobs I've applied for.'

'What jobs?'

'Duh! That's why you gotta help think of some I might've applied for.'

'How do I know? I don't know anyone that works. Just write in that space you didn't spot anything to apply for.'

'Yeah. Anyway, my knees hurt.' He stood on one leg, bent the other back until it clicked, then did the other. Meanwhile, Dawn told him everything she'd done that week.

Gary looked pleased when she'd said she'd found a way around the bed problem.

'So I can doss at yours?'

'I'll ask Ma in a bit. But we need to get our own place, have a baby, be a unit.'

'Unit - yeah?'

She giggled, putting a hand in his pocket while they strolled on.

The park had a couple of benches that weren't broken. They shoved off a homeless bloke so they could sit and have a smoke while they waited for a few mates. It was September, so most of them were shot of school and waiting for apprenticeships. There were hardly any available, so no real worry about getting tied up. Kaylee reckoned without an apprenticeship you got a college place, and you hardly ever needed to turn up there.

Dawn didn't say a word until Gary's smoke was finished. She watched the glow disappear. He took a last draw, then looked both ways expecting their mates to come into view. They didn't. They were late.

'So, you fallen then?' he said.

Dawn giggled again. 'Took your time to cotton on, Dad, didn't you? Speedy Gonzalez.'

Gary gawped at her. 'Speedy who? You up the alley then?'

'We'll get our own place, now.'

'You're mental.'

'Well, after a bit.'

Dawn reckoned Gary was pleased. She crossed her arms, tucking her hands into her inside pockets. He hadn't said she needed an abortion or accused her of having it off with one of the others.

'It'll have to be a night bird. Babies wake in the night. So it can fucking well sleep in the morning, like me.'

She giggled. She rattled on about the news: what everyone would say, who to tell first, who was already pregnant, who'd gone for termination. Gary listened, lids halfway down.

He said, 'It'd better be bigger than Nobby's. You better have a big one. I don't want no runt.'

You could tell he was bucked. *Daddy Gary!* Dawn laughed and nudged, laughed and nudged.

'Give over, bitch.'

'Look they're coming now. Who's got some cans? Gonna tell them. Celebrate.'

Gary stood up to high-five his mates. He strode to and fro, shoulders swaying one way, then the other. His knees must've stopped hurting. The guys all stood on the path so people had to go on the grass to get by. If anyone gave them a look, they got an earful.

The girls sat round Dawn, twisting round to laugh when the guys did.

She told them.

They all nodded. 'Yeah, thought so,' and they quarrelled about the number of weeks Dawn had gone and how many times you had it off before you got knocked up.

'Becca Tonks. First time,' Cilla said.

Everyone sneered. 'Tell me another.'

'Bet your bump won't fit under the school desk!' Kaylee was always good for a laugh.

It wouldn't be worth going back to school now. She told them.

They conferred about that.

'It's not as though you were going to get any passes.'

'Who says?' Dawn answered.

They all cackled like old witches.

'But you'll have to keep going into school until you have it.'

'Haven't gone in much this term. I'll just say I've got labour pains. They won't know. I can't go in when it's due, anyway. They won't want a birth in Maths, Set Three.'

'Imagine Mr Kelvin, delivering it!'

They all fell about.

Kaylee yelped. 'Even in the medical room!'

Cilla was practical. 'When you can't get to school, you get home tuition.'

Dawn gasped, 'Wha?'

'Yeah, you'll have to—fifteen.'

'I'll be sixteen by the time it comes.'

'Still. Home tuition like Becca Tonks. She done a GCSE. And it keeps on after you have the baby, then you go to college.'

Gary leaned forward, head between the girls' shoulders. 'I'm not having you leave the baby and go to college.'

Kaylee nudged him. 'Don't you want her educated?'

'Not if I get left with the baby.'

'Anyway, I'm educated enough.' Dawn knew her own mind.

Georgaline said, 'Better to rest up first, let the baby get real big.'

'Yeah.' Dawn agreed.

But first she had to tell Ma. Gary living with them in their one-bed flat. Ma had to get used to the idea.

They couldn't find Gary when the baby pushed out at last. He'd gone up the hospital with her, but after a bit - Dawn in bed, just waiting - he'd got restless. He'd gone off.

'My bloke's gone off!' she complained to the nurses. They'd already sent Ma off home because they'd thought two birth-partners too many.

'So now I've got sod all! Typical!'

But she had two nurses. 'We have a policy to protect ourselves against aggression.'

Dawn had taken all the dope they'd offered. Not much, for crying out loud. And crying out loud was what it made you do. They gave you a prick in the bum, eventually, when you really screamed and yelled, and some fucking mask over your face at the end. It smelled of rubber and had been over someone else's mush a few minutes before.

'Do your breathing,' they said.

'Wha'?'

'How you were shown in ante-natal class.'

She hadn't bothered with that stuff. Creepy.

They'd said she should have gone. It would have helped her, and now she was finding that out too late.

She didn't swear at them much, only yelled, 'Give me that jab, then. I need painkillers.'

No-one to hold her hand! This wasn't funny and she couldn't stop things happening. It was coming! The nurse shoved the mask over her screaming mouth.

You got a cup of tea when you woke up. There was only one other girl in the ward without curtains round, and she was pretty quiet. Her baby was in the nursery. Dawn's was in the cot nearby. She'd had a good look after it was born. Cute. 'Quite a size,' the nurses said. Gary would like that, something big he'd produced.

He should be here! He must've gone to see the council about being re-housed. Now he was eighteen he was the man of the house, or at least the flat. Ma should be grateful. Maybe he'd got lucky. Otherwise, he'd be here right now to see the baby. He'd be shown the little face, all crinkly, quite sweet really. The nurses would say, 'Look, Daddy,' and hold up the saggy white bundle, like a bag of sugar. Probably it could be called Sugar. See what Gary thought.

She wanted to see Gary's face. A father! That'd show him.

Being underage meant a social worker poking her nose in. But when she called round, Gary had acted posh and said he was a job-seeker, and Ma said she'd do any support parenting, so the social worker went away. She could sod off to the losers who couldn't manage their lives.

While Dawn was waiting for Gary, the midwife started the baby off on the breast. Silly really. It had only just come out. Why would it want a drink straight away? Anyway, the baby hadn't the first idea and its eyes were closed. Dawn closed hers. She needed a rest and…something.

She hoped Gary hadn't stopped off for puff. That would make him later still. And it wasn't fair if he had some alone. Even though she was pregnant, Gary always said it wouldn't matter if she had a draw. She'd wanted to ask at the clinic if that was okay, but they could be a bit funny. Like you had only one thought in your mind, *babies*. She hadn't used much glad stuff, it wasn't as though she was one of these irresponsible slags. And anyway, she couldn't do any when Ma was there. She'd like a draw now. She deserved one after going through all that birth stuff. She was bleeding!

Being pregnant was all right. People had to be careful how they treated you, and you didn't have to do much. In the last months, too big to move far, she'd watched some great box sets on the telly. Such a laugh, her mates stuck at school taking exams or skiving off and getting stick! She was off school, legit. The home tutor was a drag but the flat was so crowded she said it would be easier if she just left *assignments,* and marked them at home. Ma and Gary did bits of them together. Dawn wouldn't join in, she did her mindful colouring when they were at it. None of them bothered reading the marked work and the tutor said she was rather disappointed with Dawn's progress. Gary said it proved Dawn wasn't as brainy as him. She said they were his marks and she was brainier for not being stupid enough to do any.

The nurses were nice to you when you were in labour, even if they got up-tight and bossy. They got you a jug of orange. You felt quite important.

Mind you, it fucking hurt. She'd tell Gary that. She'd said to him a few months ago, 'Bet it hurts.' And he'd said 'Naw. Nothing to it. Natural in'i?' Anyway, she had to like this getting pregnant stuff, people waiting on you. She'd need to have at least one more baby before they got a place of their own, separate from Ma. Sherreen had to have three kids before she'd got that two-bed flat over The Black Dog. God!

Dawn thought she might quite like being a mother. People had to notice you. You had something to show off. People came round to see it, and you pushed it up and down the street in a buggy, all dressed up.

After Dawn's nap, an orderly came round with the trolley. Quite decent sausage and mash, sponge pud, coffee, roll and butter, cheese wrapped up in see-through stuff; all clean.

The girl in the next bed didn't want her dinner so she gave it to Dawn. Dawn was hungry enough to eat two, so she did. It was free. She hid the rolls and cheese in her bag to give Gary when he came. She bet he'd spent everything on puff and wouldn't be hungry. But she'd make him eat. And he'd leave a draw for when she got down the bathroom. She'd open the window and no-one would know.

Hey, one of these women here might like a joint. Gary could make a bit of extra dosh when the nurses weren't looking. Or perhaps they also… no, too risky.

The baby was crying - ever such a funny noise. Like that cat outside next door's. Dawn hoped the baby wouldn't do it often.

Ma would like the baby. So much for all the fuss she'd made when Dawn had—not told her exactly, more, let Ma notice. Her grandchild. Now Ma had something of Gary's too.

He'd told her, the three of them squashed on the sofa watching Goggle Box, 'Ma! My kid will be your grandchild,' and gave his wonky grin. Ma had been too emotional to say anything. Anyway, she'd probably worked that out already.

Ma stopped dead. If that wasn't Gary, it was his double. Lying up an alley on his back, arms spread out, as though on a beach in the Bahamas.

She'd better go and check. She put her shopping down a few yards away and sidled up gingerly. If it wasn't Gary, the bloke might have a go at her. If it was Gary, he might have a go at her and all, the state he looked in. Heaven's sake! His little baby all new and waiting in the hospital for him and poor Dawnie gone through her labour without him. Ma leaned over. Although his head was lolled the other way, she recognized the hell's mouth buckle on his belt.

'Gary! Get up. The baby's born. Dawn's waiting for you up the hospital,' but Ma could see that Gary was out of it. Could she get someone who'd be all right about helping to get him home and off the street? But it couldn't be just anyone. She didn't want Gary shopped; Dawn needed him. She pulled at Gary's denims but he hardly opened his eyes. After her more aggressive pull at his belt, he leant back on the kerb with a gormless leer. He obviously wasn't capable of walking. Help!

But someone was lurching up the alley—a bloke, a teenager. She gave him a quick look. He seemed reasonably with it, so she asked if he knew Gary.

'Yeah. Def. Know the story. Someone's just offered him their big bedsit. Private let. They had to get out quick. He didn't have to palm anyone so he bought a poor man's speedball. Said it was his last before becoming a father!'

'His baby's born. He should be down the hospital with Dawn.'

The bloke chortled. 'So he already was a father! The laugh's on him. My mate's back there. We'll haul the dude back home before the fuzz come. That's what friends are for.' He put one hand in Gary's jeans and found a tenner.

Ma didn't say anything when he shoved it in his pocket.

When he hoisted Gary up, she went straight back to her daughter. Someone had to.

Dawn said, 'Aw, it's you Ma. I want Gary. What you doing here again? The nurse said you'd seen the baby.'

Ma looked a bit down. She should be over the moon, now she was a Grandma. 'You should be over the moon, not with a bloody long face like that. Here,' and Dawn passed over the bundle.

'She's quite sweet. We might call her Sugar, depending what Gary says. He don't even know it's a girl yet. Where the hell is he?'

Ma said 'He's out.' She liked to stick as near to the truth as possible. She took the baby and held her tight, looking at her real close. 'What was the name of that friend of yours? That one who got caught in the Spar with six bottles of whisky under her tent coat and the *Upmarket Fashions* ticket still on it?'

'Oh. Bin.'

'Bin? What's that short for, then?'

' 'S'not. She used to get her needles out the bins so we called her that. Don't know any other name for her. She's not a friend. I just know her. She had a girl a year or more ago.'

'Yes. I remember. She used to bring it into the supermarket, screaming. I held her sometimes when I was on shelves. Seemed fairer to the other customers.' Ma was still looking closely at Sugar.

Dawn thought Ma was a bit off, not being emotional about her grandchild. Bin's Ma had cried, off and on, for a week. "Overwhelmed," Bin said. But Bin's mother often had tears down her face or starting in her eyes. Scrappy little baby, Bin's. Too much crack in it. Had the shivers for weeks before it was allowed home. Dawn's was all right. Crying, but not shivering. She said pointedly to Ma, 'The nurse said she was lovely.'

Ma said, 'She is. Thanks to the rest you had, and the vitamins.'

Dawn wasn't good on thanks.

Ma was still peering at Sugar. She said slowly, 'Bit like Bin's, isn't she?'

'No!' Dawn asked her if she wanted to fall out. Sometimes she got so mad at Ma and it wasn't easy holding it in. But the stroppy nurse was in the room. Dawn poked Ma. 'Have you seen Gary? He should be here, for crying out loud. Has he got anywhere with the housing?'

Ma said, 'I think something might be coming up.'

'I don't mind what it is, I'm not stopping at yours, the three of us. Cramps our style. No privacy.'

Ma agreed, and rocked the baby.

Dawn thought she'd make the best of it while she was in here.

Meals got brought to you. Hospital was comfortable. She'd been through the trauma of childbirth and now she needed rest.

The nurses agreed with Ma. Because of Dawn's age and the tiny flat, it was best she stayed put for a few days. 'Lots to learn.'

So Dawn lay back. The telly was on. It wouldn't be long before Gary came.

Two days later, he did, but the rolls were hard and the butter squelchy, so she ditched them.

~

The baby was a month old, now, and her cries were getting loud enough to stop Ma sleeping the days Sugar was left with her. She was on her way back from the supermarket. Her back was aching. She'd been doing overtime on the shelves. Babies cost ever such a lot. It wouldn't hurt Gary to fork out for a change, but he'd had no luck getting any work. At least, that's what he said each week when she asked.

It was going to be a tight thing, helping them out in their bed-sit, but if she didn't, who would? It would be the baby who suffered. There was no heat in that shitty house, February and all. They needed at least four more tokens every week for the meter.

The shopping was heavy and her ankles were swollen. Just another two streets and two corners... oh my! A ranging dog, loping and barking, and ambling footsteps behind her announced Gary's arrival.

'Or righ' ?' he said, not meaning any enquiry.

If he looked, he could see that she wasn't all right and would notice the heavy bags. But he didn't look.

'Any luck, Gary?'

'Wha'?'

'Down the Job Centre?'

'Oh. Ah. Naw. Nothing that fits my skills. A bitch in'it?' He took a sudden interest in the shopping bags. 'Oh - you get that baby milk? Just remembered, Dawn said to get it on me way back.'

Ma held out a bag invitingly. 'Yes, I did, and how about you help me carry it?'

'Uh?' He looked at the bags a moment before he took hold of one. Gary was no gentleman. Phil used to wait in the pub until she finished the shopping, then buy her a pint and it was him carried the shopping home. Nice, in those days, before the later blokes, way back before Dawnie.

Dawnie hadn't felt very energetic since she came back from hospital. She said it was a waste not to read those magazines her visitors had brought. 'It's best I take a rest., Ma.'

Having a baby wears you out, specially your first, and Dawnie was still Ma's baby.

∽

It was all right in the bed-sit. Now they were a family. While Dawn was getting over the birth, Gary and Ma had moved all their gear in. It filled all of Ma's carrier bags, seven bin liners and the sports bag Dawnie's ex- (Year Eleven) left behind last year.

Ma said the place had been left like a hell-hole. It had taken her days getting it clean enough for a baby to live in.

Demon liked it in the new place. You let him out over the industrial site opposite and and he could do all his barking there; no-one to complain or tell you to use doggie bags. Then Dawn could sit on the sofa without Demon, and stick Sugar on it between feeds.

Dawn pulled out another teat from the hospital bounty bag full of ointments and juice and nappies and bottle steriliser, and things Dawn hadn't got round to buying beforehand. The Absorbatot nappies lasted brill. They let the wet soak through to the back so the top still looked dry and if you turned them around you could use the dry bit next time. You put one on in the morning and it was still not too pongy at night. Even next day... though normally Dawn changed Sugar by then because she liked to keep her nice.

They'd had a ball after she got home, everyone visiting, plenty of booze and that. Ma and people had given them stuff for their new place, and the baby had presents from everyone. Dawn had dressed Sugar up lovely, Sugar Pink everyone said. Gary got pissed, but everyone said it was his privilege to wet the baby's head.

Yeah. Gary'd been so long getting to see Sugar when she was born! He'd been knocked out with the thrill. Bless Him. While she was busy giving birth, Gary was finding them their own place. Then he stoked himself against the shock of being a father, you couldn't criticize that. Gary was sensitive, couldn't take things, emotionally. He had to use puff to cope. She liked that, a sensitive man. Full of feelings. She didn't want no block of stone.

Gary'd had a downer after he'd been to see her and Sugar that first time. He'd felt awful tired. Then helping Ma move all their stuff to the bedsit. He hadn't any energy to go down the Job Centre after. Who could blame him? Dawn was glad really. The last thing she wanted was Gary starting work just when she needed him to lend a hand. After all, if he'd been employed, they'd have given him paternity leave so it was only right he took it now, sort of.

~

Sugar turned out to be not so sweet. She cried and pooed and even sicked-up. Life was all feeds and lots of washing. It was Gary's baby too. Dawn wasn't going to be stuck with all the work. Gary would have to do his share.

Trouble was, he said, he'd been head-hunted by a warehouse who wanted him as an operative and the Job Centre said he had to take it or lose his income-based benefit. He was going to be out sixteen bloody hours every week.

The Health Visitor came quite a bit, even when Gary was home, and nagged a lot. What a fuss! The woman didn't like the ash-trays full, she didn't like the way Gary held Sugar by one arm, she didn't like the baby bottles put where the dog was, she didn't like Sugar on the sofa, especially if Dawn was over the landing with her neighbour. What did she think—that Sugar would run away?

It was when the Health Visitor threw away the sterilising liquid that Dawn saw red. She'd only put new in a few days before. *And* it was the bottle Dawn had bought herself. Just because there were dog hairs in it! Not surprising Dawn couldn't mind her language.

The woman had the cheek to tell Dawn not to smoke when Sugar was propped up for her feed. 'You could actually hold her, and go outside for your cigarette after her feed, surely?'

Fuck that! As if Sugar minded! She had her bottle, what did she care what Dawn did? She wasn't even looking.

After that, when the Health Visitor was due, Gary would say, 'If she's coming, I'm off!' so Dawn was stuck alone with her nagging. It wasn't fair.

Gary wasn't getting up in the night either. Dawn had a go at him. 'Before Sugar come, you fucking said you'd do the night one!'

'Yeah, but I'm working now! I'm no good when I'm knackered. Anyway, I did one this afternoon when you were doing yer club round. Sugar gets fed evenings and when we turn in. If she wails after, it won't hurt her to wait till morning. Spoils kids if you give in to them the minute they yowl.'

'But she don't stop! Then I have to fucking do it!'

'So! Your Ma usually does the day ones.'

'You got to take your turn, Gary. You're the Dad and you said you would.'

Every night they argued until one of them got sick of Sugar's noise and leaned out of bed to stick the teat in her mouth. Once, Gary picked up the wrong bottle. It was the one she'd finished the feed before, and Sugar just sucked at the empty bottle until she fell asleep. In the morning, when they realised, they had such a laugh about that.

～

Three months in and Ma could see Dawn hadn't got the hang of mothering yet. Well, she wouldn't, with it being her first. And she was still a kid herself, let's face it. Dawnie didn't really notice when Sugar needed seeing to, so Ma did it. She should show Dawnie how to do things, which meant going round their place a lot.

Gary? He was better. He could do it, but would he? By the time he got off the chair to see to Sugar, she'd cried herself into such a strop it took twenty minutes to soothe her, and by that time she'd dropped off without her feed, poor little thing.

Then the benefits situation. This Universal Credit—how were any of them going to understand the ins and outs? All those forms!

The warehouse said they could manage without Gary, and he said he'd been offered a job that better suited his skills, though Ma couldn't see what skills were needed to put labels on beer barrels and count them onto the vans. It gave him more hours' work, but it meant he wasn't around much for Sugar's care.

Lately, he'd been texting and even phoning her. 'You're not seeing much of Sugar, Ma. You ought to. You're her Granny.'

She was miffed. 'I *am* around, every day, straight after my early shift, but you're still asleep then.'

His hours were three till eight; twenty-five hours a week. Ma supposed she was lucky Gary didn't mind her visiting Dawnie. Some mothers-in-law were frozen out.

Each time she got to their place, Sugar was wet, sticky, crying, and their bedsit was in a real state. Dawnie got mad if Ma criticised.

'It's my work what stops me!'

Yes, Dawnie had started a little job, selling cosmetics to women in their homes, just on occasion, on a dry afternoon. She called it work experience for her college course, not that she went there often. When Dawn was out but Gary in, Ma shouldn't need to be there, but what to do for the best? Sugar would be in the cot, Gary sprawled on the settee the worse for wear. She wouldn't know whether it was drink or the other thing. Eventually, Ma spoke straight. 'Look Gary...'

'Whaaa? I'm knackered after work. Obvious, in'i.'

'But Gary, I can't always be here. I've got work too. What would happen if Sugar was bad and you was like this?'

'So! This is your baby is it?' He pulled himself off the sofa, stood over her so close she could smell his stale sweat and beer. 'You getting at me because you lent us that money? I said you'll get it all back and you will, every penny, Scrooge. You're so unreasonable. I allow you here, no limits, see Dawn and the baby whenever you want so you're not lonely, and this is what I get!'

Best not to say anything and just see to Sugar. Sugar gurgled and smiled at her. Who wouldn't feel better?

Dawnie was calmer too, when Sugar was cleaned up and smiling. 'You do it nice, Ma. Don't go on at Gary. He's all man. He don't have a way with babies like we do.'

As the weeks went by, Dawn found it better to leave the baby at Ma's, evenings, while they went clubbing or whatever, and then, in the afternoons too, 'since you're having her tonight anyway.'

With Sugar so often left at her place, Ma didn't need to go round to Dawnie's much.

Gary said it was all work for him, now the benefits situation was changing. 'It always pays to work, Ma, see? So we have to leave Sugar with you. We've tried hard to fit it in with your shifts, y'know.'

Dawn preened herself in front of the full-length mirror they'd carried down all those streets. *Freecycle* was magic. Six months on and she had her figure back. It'd been gross when she was fatter than the geeks who stayed on at school to do 'A' levels.

Flaming nuisance, the Health Visitor was still nagging and calling round. Often they were out, or out of it. Sometimes they weren't, but they didn't bother answering the door if they knew it was her.

They were caught out once because they were expecting the pizza man. With the door open, Dawn couldn't help the Health Visitor walking in. She held Sugar and weighed her and said Sugar wasn't doing too well.

(So Ma couldn't have been doing a good job, but Dawn didn't say so.)

The Health Visitor needed to understand what it was like, Sugar being as she was. 'Well, I'm always feeding her. But when they're sick all the time what can you do?'

The Health Visitor's answer went on and on. All sorts of things she expected Dawn to be doing. Shit! Who did she think she was, ordering someone about in her own home. She put the woman right: 'Anyway, she's my baby, I have the say.'

~

A week or so later they found a new social worker on the doorstep when they got back from the Benefits place. Cheek! She asked if Dawn would like someone to help her learn parenting skills.

'Not really,' said Dawn. 'It comes natural when you have a baby. You'll know when you have one yourself.'

Gary liked that attitude. He took Dawn upstairs and gave her one.

~

Now she was pregnant again, they'd get a better place, bound to. When she'd waved the pee stick at Gary, he'd gone straight down to apply.

If they had a flat, they wouldn't hear Sugar screaming so much. They often shut her buggy in the bathroom, but you could still hear her. Ma often had Sugar. That's what grandparents were for.

Dawn was cheesed off because Sugar was getting to look like Bin's scrappy baby. Ma had said that from the beginning. She shouldn't have said, because Dawn might not have noticed otherwise. Now she had. And it put her right off Sugar, so it was better if Ma had her more.

Dawn lay on the settee and turned on East Enders. Pregnant; she should put her feet up.

The phone rang, the landline. She leant over the arm of the sofa to grab it. 'Yeah?'

'Hi? Is Gary there?'

'No. Why? Who wants him?'

'Oh is that his sister? This is his girlfriend, Sasha Leigh.'

'Wha....? Who...?'

'He said he'd be round here by three, and I thought ...'

'Well think again, bitch. NO, this isn't his sister. THIS is his girlfriend, his PARTNER, the Mother of his Baby.'

'What baby? It's my baby...'

'Wha-at! Sugar! I had her in St Joseph's. What d'yer mean?'

'Damien! I had him in the General.'

Dawn had plenty to say after that, in words unprintable.

After Dawn told Sasha Leigh what to do with Damien, she rang Ma and was on the phone sounding off, right until Ma said to cool off and think of her pregnancy. So Dawn went down The Red Whistle. Gary wasn't there, so she had a few vodka cokes to lift her spirits.

When she went to collect Sugar, Ma had already told Gary about Sasha Leigh's call. Obviously, he wouldn't be quick coming home now! Dawn reckoned he'd make for the Black Dog which was the furthest away. She was right. She caught him on the way and kicked him good and hard and gonged him on the head with the parasol from Sugar's buggy.

Then Gary went on down the Black Dog and got plastered. He went up Bin's to sleep it off.

A week later, when he came back, Gary didn't say nothing about Sasha Leigh and Damien. Dawn had her arms folded and all the cash hidden away amongst the new packs of LadyLove Face Fresheners where he'd never find it. He needn't think he was going to have anything from her except a bad time.

'O'right?' He was all smiles. 'D'yer want the good news or the good news?'

She didn't clock him one after all, in case he'd fixed a flat for them somehow. 'Wha' then?'

'The Social was round Bin's because she got done for shop-lifting and this time they say she'll get a stretch. They was going to put the kid in Care, but I said I was the father visiting my child and would take it over.'

'You what? What did you say that for?' Dawn could be a bit slow.

'It's got Special Needs, you stupid cow. More benefit! With your new one and Sugar as well, we'll get lots of points. They'll give us a two-bed, def. And you'll get an attendance allowance. Am I a quick thinker or what?'

Gary was brilliant, even if he was a sod. 'Me, look after your fucking kid? Think I'm a saint?' But it would save Dawn having to plan a third.

Gary flicked his hair back. 'Forget the father bit. I only did it with Bin once. Silly cow had no condoms. We were never together.'

'So. Where's the kid now?'

'I wheeled her down your Ma's. I told her about the benefits and she took the buggy indoors.'

On the whole, Dawn was glad about this new turn of events although it would mean a lot of work for Ma. She stopped feeling daggers about Gary and Bin when she thought how much extra the allowances would be. She got out the Christmas bottle of Baileys to celebrate.

While Gary was up Bin's, Ma found out he had babies all over the place. 'Jeez, Dawnie, what have you got yourself into?' Ma had got herself in a stew.

'Gary can't help it, Ma, bless him. With his phys*ique*... He's all man. You got to expect it when you collar the best lay. Look at celebrities. All the hunks have kids everywhere.'

Ma went on about Bin's scrappy kid and the extra work. 'She's quiet, mind. What's she called?'

'Er - forgotten. Anyhow, you can call it what you want, it won't know.'

Ma rubbed her forehead. 'And what about the other girls?'

'Forget them. They've put Father Unknown. Gary told them as a single parent they'd get more benefit, and it's safer. It's only Sasha Leigh who's *said,* stupid bitch.' She shut her eyes, shut her mind to Gary going up the Contact Centre twice a month.

Dawn thought about having Bin's kid. Lynne, she'd call it, to rhyme with Bin. Lynne, being that bit older, could soon help out with Sugar, as well as the new one. Ma would be fine with all of them - she'd love it.

Dawn brought her cosmetics in and stacked them in the free corner. Gary was seeing his workmates out. The match was over. He hadn't let them smoke in the room because of Sugar being there! The guys had been talking about work. Gary was one of the workers; you had to be impressed.

'O-right, doll?'

She looked at the empties. Gary took them off. He was proper house-trained. Then he came back and plonked himself on the bed-chair they'd got from the *Families in Need* shop.

'Legal phoned. Bin's case done. She got a year.'

Ha! Bin inside and serving time; serve her right. Dawn, big-bellied, taking over Bin's scrawny kid, the social would rate her. They'd say, "That's very generous of you." She and Gary would be Dad and Mum to a big family. That'd show Sasha Leigh who Gary belonged to!

Later, Ma brought Lynne over. She put a bag of stuff Gary had found for Lynne in Bin's dump, then left. 'I got to clear up my own place, now.'

Dawn gave Lynne a dummy and sat her in the playpen.

Sugar was on the sofa. She dressed her up in new clothes, the pink flamingo blouse and over tunic. They'd been in Lynne's bag but they'd look nicer on Sugar.

Dawn's mind was in overtime. Three kids and you nearly always got a house, particularly with a Special Needs kid. They couldn't leave her in a bed-sit with three babies! A three-bed semi down Arbutt Road would do just fine. She lay Sugar down, stuck a bottle in Lynne's mouth and leant over to give Gary a plonker on his mouth. He took out his draw and smirked.

They watched East Enders, then Coronation Street. They thought about watching the lions on David Attenborough's latest.

Gary said, 'It'd look better if we had a 64 inch screen. We'd be able to see right down its jaws.'

She said, 'You going up the council then?'

He pulled himself up, his knees cracking with the effort. 'Yeah, I'm off up there. I'm the one makes things happen, doll.' He went out so fast the video rack rattled.

Sugar let out a cry. Lynne copied.

Dawn knew that discipline worked. She shook a fist at Sugar. 'That's enough, you. And Lynne, you got your bottle, so shut it.'

The downstairs door slammed, Gary's whistle echoed down the alley. Sugar only moaned a little while. She'd wait a bit for her solids. Just in case she didn't, Dawn took Sugar into the bathroom and shut the door on her. They really needed more than one room for everything.

On the telly, a playback of Tuesday's episode of *Jaytown* began. Everyone said she shouldn't have missed it. The younger sister with the burnt hair went for her teacher with her nails. Epic. Dawn put her fluffy slippers up and leant back to enjoy it, nice and comfy. The gang might come round soon, probably with a few cans.

Dawn's dreams were going to come true. Her Gary was a man of action. He was going to collar that semi. When she saw the house, Ma would say "I knew you two would make it!" They'd have a shared alley to the back garden with a plastic slide, and hard-standing for Gary's motor-bikes and chains. On Benefits day, Dawn would take the cheque and go up the Mall to spend it, pushing the buggy with two babies in it and one hanging on.

People would say, "I don't know how you do it!" And Dawn could say "Well... Lynne's mum's in prison, drugs, neglect. Poor kid's been deprived. Someone's got to give her a good home."

After the soap, Dawn dropped off to sleep and only woke with a start when she heard the bike slam down and the usual kick to the dustbins. Gary. The kick was his way of saying, 'I'm home, lover.'

Had he been to some farm? Gary's boots trod so much muck onto the mat you couldn't see it was orange anymore. She was buggered if she'd clean it up.

He stuck his chin forward at her and grabbed a handful of jelly babies off the table. 'I've had it up to here. They won't fucking do it, even when I threatened with phoning our MP.'

'Our wha-?'

'The bloke you phone when you got complaints with the council or neighbours. They say we 'an't got enough points. They say Lynne in't yours and Bin'll want her as soon as she's done her time. You'll have to think of something else. Anyway, your baby's screaming her head off in the bathroom while you sit here mooning.'

Ma went up Dawn's quickish. She hadn't seen them for a bit and Dawn was in a right mood with her for not babysitting. They'd had to take Sugar and Lynne up the pub with them three nights on the go. Anyway, it was better if she told them the news now, get it over with.

Luckily, Dawn was in on her own.

'Dawnie? How are you, my special girl? And where's my little treasure?' She picked Sugar up quickly and dabbed her face. 'Crying?'

'Probably forgotten who you are. She hasn't seen you for an age. She ought to cry. Where you been?'

'Problems.'

'Tell me about it! What about me? Council turning Gary down. Us lot stuck here, eh?' Dawnie wasn't what you'd call a listener.

Ma covered Lynne up, her legs were bare and mottled. She put the kettle on, made tea. Dawn lolled back on the sofa. Ma brought a mug over and stood it on the Argos catalogue.

'Look, Dawn. You know there was another bloke before your Dad?'

'And one after, or two. Good riddance.'

'Well, Rick's been back. Like old times, before I had you.'

Dawnie groaned. 'Dinosaur.'

'He's been back a while but I knew you wouldn't like it, so that's why I haven't been round. He's been up mine a lot of the time. He didn't want me tied up with the baby, let alone two. Anyway, just as I got used to him again, he's gone.'

'Huh. So?'

'Well, he's left something behind.'

Dawn stretched out an open hand. 'Come round to share it?'

Ma shook her head and snorted. 'No such luck.' She patted her stomach.

Dawn said, 'Whatcha mean?' But, given a few moments' thought, even Dawn could work out what that meant. 'Ma-a-a—you can't!' Her eyes goggled like prize marbles. 'No!'

'Why not?'

'You're old. You're my Mum. Gross!'

'That woman in the news was sixty, having hers. I'm only just forty.'

'But Ma! That's shit! Yours'd be younger than mine. And I'd have a sister younger than Sugar—'

'Or brother. Looking after Sugar's got me quite back into babies, even if Rick has sodded off.'

'That's probably why. Ma-a-a! This is a fucking fuck of a day. You've not been no help, and us stuck in this bed-sit forever.'

'Listen. Sugar won't mind. They'll all play together nice; Sugar, Lynne, your new baby, and mine. Lovely. About time I looked after a baby of my own.'

'What? You got me.' Dawn drank her tea without another word. Ma hoped it wouldn't be a long sulk, like for days.

Gary came in with a swagger. He was a brewery operative,

permanent. 'O-right, Ma? Come for Sugar? 'Bout time we had some babysitting, eh.'

She told him her news. He stayed standing up, looking her up and down. 'Why weren't you careful, at your age?'

It was Rick wasn't careful. She shouldn't have trusted him. She wasn't going to discuss that sort of thing with Gary. She passed Sugar to him, sort of diversion. 'Here's Daddy, sweetheart.'

Sugar looked back at her and held out one little arm.

Gary said, 'See, she wants a sleepover at Granny's.'

'It's awkward, Gary. That's the other thing I got to tell you two. The landlord. He's done his annual inspection of our place. I had mine all neat, but them upstairs made complaints about Sugar crying. He reminded me of my lease—no kids or pets. I only had Dawnie, and she was twelve, when I got the place. I told him Sugar hadn't been round recently but I had to let him know a new baby's on the way. He's given me three months notice.'

Dawn screeched. 'Can't have the babies at yours?'

Gary turned the telly off. He knew this was serious. He rubbed a thumb up and down his stubble. 'How we going to manage if you don't never have Sugar at yours, or Lynne?'

Lynne waved a feeble arm, her near-empty bottle dripping milky tears.

'And if you get evicted, Ma, you'll be homeless,' Dawn nodded meaningfully, 'unless you can move in with your bloke. Or someone.'

Ma put her head in her hands. 'No, I got no-one. Shit! What am I going to do?'

Dawnie lay her head sideways on the cushion. 'Can't you follow after whatsisname? It's his kid, going to be.'

She should have known Dawnie wouldn't help. 'Course not. He's buggered way off. Got a kiosk on the Costa del Sol with his mate. I've worked out, he was only marking time being at my place until his business got set up.'

Gary walked up and down between the buggy and the new sound woofer, Sugar hanging over one of his elbows. 'I'm thinking.'

She and Dawn waited. He was the man, after all, even if he

was a waster. Without the telly, the room was so quiet you could hear the motorway traffic pounding away. Then he turned to face the sofa with both of them on it, side by side, looking up at him.

'Dawn, where's your iPhone what you got off Whatshisface who thinks he's your dad?'

Dawn passed it over. 'Not much data left.'

'No prob. I'm a rapid surfer. Did the free course for job seekers and I 'an't forgotten it.' He surfed, his eyebrows going up and down like waves. Then he logged off, one side of his mouth pushed outwards.

That smile, what a winner.

'Got a solution,' he said. 'It's a fixer. You move in with us, Ma, and have the baby. Then we'll be seriously overcrowded and have loadsa points. *Council estate.*'

He tapped Dawn's iphone. 'Says it here. Three adults, two kids, we'll get a three-bed. Four kids—bloody 'ell, if I had Damien staying over, we could ask for a four-bed. Or if one of you has a boy. Can't have him sharing with the girls.'

Ma was wordless.

Dawnie sat up straight. 'You're a genius, Gary. What did I tell you, Ma, when you first met him? Come on. Stick Sugar in the buggy, I'll get Lynne from the bedroom and we'll go down that new estate - Wills Wood - and take a look at it. We might get offered one of them, all new and shimy. We don't need bloody Damien, Gary, mind.'

Ma's breath was taken away. 'You're one in a million, Gary, taking it like that. You deserve to make it, you do.'

∾

Her Gary was worth his weight in (was it bed or gold?) Anyway, Dawn had lots to think about. She'd wait until Ma had her ante-natal, then once she'd had this baby, they'd go down the council again. It was true she might have a boy this time—not that she was going to let them do that needle thing and tell her boy or girl. She hadn't last time. Hey, suppose she pretended she *knew* it was going to be a boy? How would they know different? If it was a boy, she'd call it Caspian, like that series on Sky One. Otherwise, it could be Sweetie, to go with Sugar.

Ma could call hers Rick or Mary for all Dawn cared. She wasn't going to like the kid, whatever it was, and there was no way she was going to babysit. What! The point was, whatever Ma had, it would get them points. And because Ma was so old, her kid might have something wrong with it, and that'd be more points. Then the Council would have to give them a house quick.

If they got stuck with all girls (they'd never, surely?) If Bin failed her parole, and no way would she be making it easy for the pigs to control her, Lynne had to stay here. Anyway, Dawn'd tell the council how difficult it was getting Lynne's buggy down the steps, Lynne being so big now, and still not walking. Then they might get the house before Ma's baby came. After it, Ma would be on the spot to look after all the kids.

But Dawn couldn't work out where Ma and her baby would move after they'd got the house. They wouldn't want her there for long... but Ma wouldn't want to move from a three or four-bed house. How could she get Ma out, after?

...Unless she could say Ma's baby was Gary's. Yeah! Serve him right for saying he was brainier than her! Dawn still had that social worker's number. She'd said, 'Best keep my card, in case.' And Gary took it. That *figurine* Ma had given them for Christmas. a nude woman bending down. Gary stuck the card in its bum crack. It was still there. When the time came, Dawn would phone that social worker. She'd understand how Dawn was so upset, how she couldn't have her sister younger than her daughter (or son) AND it be her step-child at the same time. Or Gary having it off with both of them. Social workers understood this sorta problem. She'd want Ma *accommodated* somewhere else. "Inappropriate." Dawn knew their words. That's what she'd say. Otherwise...there was always the newspapers.

Dawn took the puff out of Gary's jacket. She deserved it if he'd cheated on her with Ma...even though he hadn't. She laughed. Gross, the idea!

Lynne was quiet, just lolling around in the playpen with a Peppa Pig. Sugar was playing on the floor and Demon was licking her, so it was all peaceful. Dawn lay back on the sofa and took a draw.

~

Ma wasn't looking forward to sleeping nights in a duvet behind their sofa, but it paid to be grateful when good things were going to come of it. Before any gossip started about her being kicked out by the landlord, she got in a boast to Her Next Door. 'My Dawn's a Saint, she is. She looks after her own kid, her friend's what's in trouble and now another's on the way. Her Gary's got ever such a good job in the brewery business. They're applying for a three-bed on that new estate.'

'Yeah? Lucky them.'

'Yes. But she deserves it. I always knew she'd make it.'

'But it's her Gary that's made it, in'it? Regular job. Look at him, off out every day, isn't he?'

'Nearly.'

'Twenty hours?'

'It's going to be, when his trial month's up.' Ma went back inside, smiling. That had shown Her Next Door what sort of family Ma had.

Now it was time to go and wake Gary up. If he slept past two, he'd be late for work. More, there were two babies waiting for Ma... and two more she was waiting for. That made her smile.

When the new babies came, she wouldn't be able to work any of the shifts at the supermarket. With the man of the house working all those hours, Ma couldn't leave Dawn with all the babies. She'd describe herself as a carer.

Gary hadn't been able to do much with his wandering eye and weak knees, but with child care organized, he'd be the breadwinner.

~

Gary kicked the autumn leaves to and fro on his way down the Black Dog, then a discarded Red Bull can, which was more fun.

He'd had it up to here with all that *FreeCycle* stuff to collect. It was too much after a day's work, hauling the gear from his mate's van. Both his women were near useless getting it indoors. He'd got through two smokes by the time they'd finished. Dawn was always slow, but he'd've thought Ma could do better. They both kept holding their stomachs, like the baby might fall out or sommat.

A warm fug escaped from the Black Dog's entry. He hesitated just inside the snug door. Who was up for buying him a pint? He had a quick scout around. Great, there was Darren, Sasha Leigh's new lay. You couldn't miss him, towering over the rest of the lads; twice their width too. Thick as a plank, but loose with his lolly.

'O'right, Darren?'

'Gary! Look at me 'ands.' He showed how far the black had sunk into their flesh now he was on the tarmacking.

'Yeah, but look what they pay you.'

'Yeah. Have a jar.'

'Ta, Fletcher's Gold.'

When Darren brought his pint, he asked, 'How's my son?'

'O'right, but I'm getting sick of his mother. A bleeding nag she is. Shame you can't have her down your place when it's your contact with Damien.'

Gary drew himself upright. He straightened his knees. 'My trouble is, I got too many women.'

'Too many babies! Five, isn't it?'

'Virile, I am. Can't help that.'

They drank their pints, thinking.

Gary said, 'Tell Sasha Leigh she can bring Damien up my new place. Forty-two, Heron's Way.'

'You up the new estate? Shit!'

'Brewery operative, aren't I? Got a family to support. Can't do that in a bed-sit.'

'No.' Darren splayed his blackened hands out over the table. 'Yeah, thanks, mate. It'd be better for me if you had Sasha Leigh bring Damien there. But what about Dawn?'

'I'll send her out shopping. She likes shopping. If Dawn's out, Sasha Leigh can play with my other girls while I have contact with my son. My older woman'll be in charge but she won't say nothing. She has to be careful of her Dawn's moods. Ma's like a lodger, really.'

'Sunday, then. Magic.' Darren bought Gary another pint. Heron's Way! He was proud to be mates with a bloke who had made it.

MARIAN INTERRUPTS

How reprehensible! I've been sad witness to those dysfunctional people on more than one occasion while walking Dog - I refuse to give it a name. Even with a limited social life, dog ownership means you meet people of all kinds. But some you don't speak to.

Yes, it is me, Marian. You may remember me from *Me-time Tales: tea breaks for mature women and curious men*. I am the first of the mature women, though please don't imagine 'mature' means *old*; it means sensible, fulfilled, productive.

I've adapted to being a dog owner, although furious about being landed with him by that - boy-friend! Could you call him that? Flying to a Mediterranean Isle, on his own, without inviting me, without even preparing me! And then that postcard, what a cheek! Glorying in the blue sky and gentle sea while I froze in my flat and tried to keep professionally stoic in front of my trainee managers. Worst of all, that promise he'd engineered out of me. And I don't even like dogs.

But, No, I didn't speak to Gary. We only got into a form of conversation as result of his index finger pointing accusingly at Dog's turd. While I brought out the doggie bag and wet-wipes to deal with it, he and his mates were smoking something that smelt abhorrent.

I'm glad to interrupt at this point in the book in order to introduce someone more uplifting than men who multiply procreate, lie, steal, obsess over bonfires, or cheat the benefit system.

I teach management skills, and a key part of those is self-presentation. No wonder that, should a man consider speaking to a woman, he would choose me. I know my auspicious colours and my accessories are always perfectly matched. So it wasn't a surprise to be spoken to by a man on one of those North American train marathons some holiday companies sell. Dirk was on his way home, and proved extremely pleasant company on the section ending in Edmonton.

I found his tale fascinating, and his curiosity is on a wholly different level from what you've read so far. Just try to put the last repulsive man out of your mind and read about Dirk.

THE FIND

On the stark waste of a dry crater the sculptor stands and celebrates with his three children. He wants them to witness his wilderness, but not the trauma that led him to it. For many years he'd cruised wide emptinesses alone, an unnamed mission in his heart, one he couldn't rationalise.

He's here to recapture the moment when after years of bleak, persistent searches he underwent a momentous transformation.

He doesn't speak his memories aloud. Dirk's an introverted person whose passions are private, almost secret. That's explained by an event when he was fifteen years old, the only child of research scientists specialising in the sustainability of air quality.

The Earth Sciences Conference in Toronto meant an eight-hour flight from Edmonton. Entrusting Dirk to their friends, the Watsons, his parents waved goodbye at airport security, promising to be back before his exams.

Dirk laughed. He knew the social side of the conferences was the highlight of his parents' year. If they stayed on an extra day or two, partied, took a trip with their colleagues, he didn't begrudge them the opportunity. He waved them off. 'Have fun. But I bet you're not back in time!'

He was right. They weren't back for his exams, or at all, but fragmented into space together with their plane.

Because Dirk hadn't seen the mid-air collision, it didn't seem real.

He'd been doing his homework when Mrs Watson, red-faced, hurried in and hugged him while Mr Watson, behind her, said 'Prepare yourself, son.' The hug alone announced disaster. As the Watsons gulped out the news, their words hung in the air almost visibly and remained like beings in their own right. Gentle traffic noise outside the house continued its hum, the dog went on panting, the walls remained the same colour but the mug of tea, soon placed before Dirk, tasted of dirt.

When the Watsons' two sons returned from hockey practice, their usual noise was rapidly quelled to the kind of silence called deadly. Radio and television remained switched off. Soon the quietness of the home pressed around Dirk's head, almost blinding him.

His homework books lay open on the table, just as before, so it seemed natural to continue on and on until Mrs Watson brought up his evening meal to allow him privacy.

In the following days, a study routine became his mainstay. The Watson boys treated Dirk with a paralysed kindness, passing him the best cakes with arms at their furthest extent. They lent him their treasures: X-box, magazines, books, bomber jacket, but kept their distance, like those who fear contamination. They became uncommonly polite to their parents and somewhat clingy.

Eventually, Dirk realised the lack of radio and television in the house was to protect him from news coverage of the disaster. Late at night, he heard a muttered conversation about where and to whom he should go.

'… left in trust.'

'Hardly our responsibility in truth, but…'

'We can't just pass him over to Social Services.'

'Then his grandparents will have to take him to…'

A terror gripped Dirk around his middle. Of course the Watsons needed to be shot of him. He'd been here two weeks or maybe more, he'd lost count. Where could he go? One grandmother lived in an old folks' place. The other grandparents lived in England. He'd met them twice.

The funeral was timed around their arrival day. Dirk had to make his entry trapped like a sandwich filling in an arm-in-arm three-some. He saw the crematorium was full, two journalists standing at a respectable distance behind the yew trees. The service was led with a religious fervour out of tune with his parents' beliefs; academic colleagues Dirk didn't know gave valedictions meaningless to him. Afterwards, lines of people shook his hand until its muscles ached and the skin felt rubbed raw. The dreadful afternoon, underlined by his grandmother's unrestrained grief, was a trauma he was desperate to blot from his mind.

Of course the grandparents offered Dirk a home in England; of course he refused. His final school year lay ahead. Changing his school would... He had no words to explain how it would destroy him to leave: that school, those students, those teachers, the routine, was all that kept him functioning.

He dreaded having to leave the neutrality of the Watson house. At least he knew them, knew the layout of their home, could walk from school to it, and disappear into a private bedroom after the meal. How could he bear to go to strangers even if they were relatives, let alone to a strange country, a new school?

Manfully, the Watsons hung on with their hospitality, until the grandparents finalised all legal matters. Dirk inherited his parents' house, claiming wildly, 'I'm fifteen, pretty self-sufficient. I can live at home.'

After the expected arguments and subsequent deliberations, the grandparents accepted Dirk needed to stay in his country. It was a remaining tie, he'd lost too much else. They compromised, recruiting a housekeeper to live in and care for Dirk under the Watsons' supervision, and then went back to England, grieving on many levels.

Two years passed; outside of study, a nothing time for Dirk. Hanging out with his friends only emphasised his essential difference: the absence of parental support. Most of his peers seemed inhibited in his company, terrified of unwittingly using words that might remind of the disaster. For Dirk, friends stopped being fun company. Well before graduation, Dirk rarely socialised at all.

Since his parents' death, and he must accept they were truly gone, Dirk spent time scanning the sky. It seemed the nearest guide to their present whereabouts.

He only had the Watsons to celebrate his graduation. The Watson boys ventured a 'What'll you go for?'

His parents' profession didn't appeal nor the offer of career help from the Research Institute where they'd both worked. He didn't want a sympathy place awarded him and Earth sciences seemed less relevant to him than skyward ones. More—sustainability hadn't sustained his parents so how could it sustain him?

Mr Watson said, 'Astronomy, then? You're always looking at the sky.' But Dirk wasn't captivated by what was up in space, more what came down from it, what fell. He opted for a geology degree. Where? He fancied somewhere unpeopled. Arizona, the last state to be United, away from its urban and technological centres offered mountains and wild tracts of desert.

His application to the state university was successful, and he prepared himself to become independent. He shook hands with the house-keeper, let the Watsons rent out his home and made a silent and solitary pact. He wouldn't return until he'd found… he didn't know what, but it had to be life-changing. He needed a found icon that represented what he'd lost; something no-one else had, or could have. Until he possessed such an object, he would always feel a vital part of him was missing.

He packed a mean suitcase; clothes, textbooks and papers, and one photograph. Driving seemed preferable to flying, though this took three days. He drove south to explore areas of inhospitable deserts and dramatic landscape, undaunted by the vastness of the place. For Dirk, its promise of outstretched and unimaginable terrain represented an embrace.

University provided another set of peers whose excitement at tasting independence from their parents set Dirk apart, just as being parentless had separated him from school-friends. The place was renowned for partying. So at weekends and holidays, he drove away to explore alone, reasoning this made it easier to absorb information. Arizona's canyons, deserts, rock formations, caves, colours, the very light spoke to him in a way that people could not.

During his geology studies, Dirk's interest narrowed to focus on those cosmic elements that fall to earth. After graduation, the burgeoning demand for freshly fallen meteorite material presented him with possible career opportunities. He joined a state university team analysing fragments, often the size of a pea or a grain of sand.

That year, meteorite exhibits on tour at the museum included one the size of a small cat: a carbonaceous chondrite. It had been sectioned to reveal a world of beauty under the microscope. Dirk stared at the skeletal crystals inside a single chondrule. To him it was like an aerial view of blocks of flats. He could detect eight different colours clustered like jewels, but randomly. He imagined them cities, houses within cities.

The display lacked any description of how or where the piece was found, let alone the drama of its discovery. The label stated it did not come from this planet, even this solar system, but from far beyond. Aeons earlier, it had possibly gathered material from fragments of other worlds. Even if it travelled at the speed of light, the distance and length of time it had taken to arrive was mind-blowing. Its entry to Earth, a fierce fiery flight, had fused the internal elements as close as a mother's embrace.

He peered at it until his eyes ached, gazing until the museum lights dimmed and the attendant muttered, 'Closing time'.

Dirk felt a fever of longing that he maintained in his first years of work. Life at the university seemed too safeguarded, too cosy for internal comfort. He preferred the spartan huts on the field stations.

Professor Donker led occasional meteorite excursions to well-known strewn fields. Passionate amateur hunters, often ex-marines or retirees, joined them.

Early mornings, heads down, the hunters' trek into the empty landscape began. For the others, it was a diversion, for Dirk a necessity. During most working hours he recorded the finds of others. But a find of his own, something coming involuntarily from the skies, would represent the return of matter rightfully belonging to him. Should he succeed, he didn't mean to share such a find.

On the strewn field, even tiny fragments were visible a distance away, black against the sandy expanses. One morning, the hunter nearest him spied one; his measured gait changed to an urgent run. When Donker verified the fragment as a chondrite, the sheer bliss on the hunter's face moved something inside Dirk's guts. He yearned for that experience.

'Quick, put it in here. Moist air will damage it,' Donker urged, slipping on white gloves before he guided the piece into the sealed specimen bag.

These excursions added search knowledge to Dirk's growing expertise in analysis. Before long, he began searching alone. Any find had to be solitary. Companions would wipe out its significance. His days usually ended with no success. Even without a notable find, search fever sustained him for several years. There was always a possibility. Persistence would surely lead to success?

In Arizona, late June, dry grasses bake in relentless sun, the wind picks up, clouds start rolling in. Cumulus thunderheads darken the sky until the first quenching drops of rain begin. The monsoon season has arrived, no good for searches. Dirk planned his next trip for the day immediately following its end.

With the remains of damp wind in the air, he parked illicitly and laced his boots to tramp a crater closed to the public, the site of an ancient fall.

The surface sand had dried, but areas under boulders at the crater's base showed damp residue. He scrambled down towards these and paced the uneven terrain, alert for any fragment. He lost sense of time while his eyes focussed on minute variations in the sandy terrain.

The winds in Arizona frequently halt visits to the craters. They did so on this occasion, and Dirk had a stressful climb back to the crater's rim. Not many days later, he returned. There were many more where he left empty-handed or with tiny samples unlikely to prove significant. Nevertheless, these days never seemed futile, only preparation, rehearsal.

After several search hours, one bleak and windy day, he was resting under a rigged tarpaulin and idly chewing his chunk of bread when he spotted a depression that might mark a fall. He thrust his lunch away and ran to the spot.

He pulled out his folding shovel with its attached magnet and dug down deep until he recognised the contours of a mass. Now his hands delved to grasp his find. Difficult to separate from its clay surrounds, the piece had an encouraging weightiness and when he scraped an edge, it held to the magnet. Gradually his knife pared the clay away from the piece. It was the size of his knee with thumb-sized depressions around its shiny black surface; a sure sign of fusion crust.

Manoeuvring it nearer the surface, Dirk ground an edge with his diamond file to check its composition. Carbonaceous chondrite. He knelt still, hardly breathing. His moment had come. He stopped and photographed what would seem to others just a dip in rough, sandy terrain, a clump of scarred grass blades beside it. It might become the most precious photograph he owned.

It took near to an hour before he could tug his meteorite free. As it finally became his, Dirk turned his marvel round, his hands trembling. Was this really carbonaceous chondrite, a fragment holding solar secrets from time before Earth began? He stroked its unbroken surface then covered it quickly within the specimen bag to protect it from earthly moisture. He kissed the bag, almost taking root in the time he took to fully examine its contents. Then he looked around, almost as if a posse of police might prevent his rush to escape capture.

He should use his GPS, photograph and record the find properly, return to base. But why publicise his event? The meteorite was his. He had found it alone, even if he was illicitly on this spot. He had not searched all these years to share his find. He would keep it in his rare Moroccan thuja box and only ever show it to …

Who? He had no special person to share his treasure with. What sense his mission now?

Dirk held the specimen bag to his eye level, imagining his prize piece sectioned, the myriad specks of other worlds compressed into its form. How long before he could gaze at it through a powerful microscope?

He stood, sweat pouring from his cap like lava from a volcano. A new need was replacing the years of waiting and wanting and working for this moment of possession: a need to share.

He scanned the sky and the rim of the crater as if for guidance. Was he retrieving his well-deserved personal meteorite from the desert where it fell, or stealing it away from its rightful future destiny in the state museum? Was he just a persevering thief?

Any rational professional would give Dirk the clear answer to his dilemma. He had taken, not given. His treasure had no purpose if never studied by meteoricists, or recorded and displayed for the wonder of others. What value could he put on his find without celebrating with family and friends?

It was high time he developed some.

He put his precious cargo in his backpack, photographed his coloured marker, took some bearings, and recorded the details ready to report back to the department.

The meteorite weighed him down as he bent before the wind to climb the crater. His future was uncertain, but it would not lie in the desert or the sky.

He had achieved his quest, and a new career lay ahead. His hands would not search and take, but create things memorable and lasting. He'd begin a new career. He'd become a sculptor.

He must return to Canada to begin a peopled life, colleagues, friends, wife, children. He needed a family. That revelation, he realised, was his real find.

A SWAN'S JOURNEY

My office is large, my heart is small. One of the team has just left here in tears. I refused her a day off for her aunt's funeral. An aunt - probably barren and without charm. Why would she need that young woman at her funeral? I drum my fingers on the desk.

'You should open your heart,' Andrea said, many years ago. We were reading a book together. She'd wanted first choice, but we were reading mine.

I rub the place where a heart lives. The spot feels hard and small. I blame this on never having parents to show me matters of emotion. When they died - malaria, shouldn't have taken that holiday - I was so young I could never really gain a sense of what they were like, how they looked, what we did together.

The only memory I can snatch makes little sense. Outside a bookshop, my nose on its window. "Shall we buy him a little book?" I can hear my mother's question but not summon up an image to go with it. I think a coat sleeve was beside my face, at my eye level. Then the other voice, deeper, "He has enough books for now. When he can read we'll buy him more..." and there the memory ends: the only memory I have of my parents.

For what it's worth, I've filled all my shelves with books since, even here at work. Why? I'm not going to read more than business manuals at work, but the range of books, reference, fiction, biographies, make me feel fully furnished.

An aunt and uncle took me on. "Well of course you must live here, Dan. We're your only relatives." I don't suppose that's what they actually said, but it's how I thought of it, probably in my teens.

I knew they were not thrilled to have a small child. I did not enrich their ordered life but made it poorer, as they frequently allowed me to discover.

Their squat bungalow with its two bedrooms hemmed me in without warming me up.

'We can hardly have visitors to stay, now, can we?'

'There won't be enough slack to take a holiday, now.'

'The butcher's bill seems crippling, now.'

I almost felt my name was *Now*.

But later, I think I was in junior school by then, they did have occasional dinner and bridge evenings, and one of those foursomes brought Mrs Bertha Handwick. She was a married lady with a daughter, and a civil servant husband very occupied by work and club.

Mrs Handwick approached me as I sat playing patience in the conservatory while the foursome ate dinner. It was one of the few times I remember holding any kind of conversation in the house. She decided to "give Aunt and Uncle a break," as they termed it. They could go away; I would be safely cared for. In fact, it seems Mrs Handwick had taken to me.

She took me for the week-end to her tall thin house. Seven freezing bedrooms pressed under the roof, but its large living room had a wood-burning fire, and there was an exciting range of other rooms: billiards room, music room, study, library, playroom, dining room, pantry, parlour, kitchen, even scullery, all of which I was free to explore, accompanied by her daughter, Andrea. We were both eight years old.

I always liked Andrea. From that first anxious moment when

Mrs Handwick, squeezing my chilly hand, opened the door to the living room, its blazing fire casting an orange glow on the plumped chairs, life changed. She said 'Here she is. Andrea, meet Dan. You two have fun.'

A serious child with a shiny black fringe and dark eyes looked up from her book and smiled, really smiled at me. I felt something move under my ribs. It was as if no other child had ever smiled at me, although surely some must have done.

Mrs Handwick immediately left us alone to find our own way together. We soon found we liked totally different things, but we liked each other. Andrea took me all round the house, first slowly, then at a run. Next, she tested whether I could find my way from the second floor bathroom to the billiards room, or the music room to the green bedroom, without opening a wrong door. We played hide-and-seek for quite some time. She was fascinated by hearing about my "home", the very idea of a house with only two bedrooms and a house with no upstairs. 'No stairs! That means you've never fallen down any.' And I hadn't, although I felt I'd fallen down all of Aunt's stairs.

That week-end led to others, then half-terms, then school holidays. 'You're a saint, Bertha,' glowed my aunt, transformed in her relief. 'I don't know whether it will get harder as he gets older. It's so difficult when we have absolutely no experience with children.'

'Why worry?' Mrs Handiwork's hand was a warm pressure on my left shoulder as I listened to Aunt's anxieties. 'It's our pleasure to have Dad stay, and to our benefit, in fact. It pleases Andrea so much.'

Thus I learned the reason why I went to the long, thin house with all its excitements: to give Aunt and Uncle relief, to give Andrea pleasure. I didn't care. If Andrea wanted me there, that was something wonderful. Her face always lit up when I arrived. Once, she was even kneeling at the window, waiting for me.

It didn't matter that we enjoyed different things. Normally I spent my time with Meccano. I didn't like Lego, for I had taken against plastic. I didn't like its shininess. Plastic screamed falseness to me: like women with too much make-up smiling a greasy red smile; smelly cafés with tiled walls with mispelt words on their menus. By contrast, metal was very satisfying. The Meccano pieces had holes to peer through so you could view your constructions. Screwing nuts and bolts to keep pieces in place was an anchoring thing to do.

Andrea thought Meccano was boring. She loved her dolls' house, so large with its attached garage and stables. The dolls needed clothes made for them - little pieces of material spread out on the kitchen table, or their tableware repaired - a pot of glue, a stubby glue brush. Or the furniture had to be moved when a baby was born and the bedrooms changed. The baby needed a part-time nanny, whose bedroom would be next to baby's. The big boy went away to university and his room was made into a study for the girl doll. Andrea had a script, it seemed, planned out with life events for the whole doll family. It was like the TV soap my aunt watched every evening without fail, even the time when I was brought home from school with measles. Bed (isolation) was her answer to every negative event.

I wasn't musical. Perhaps Mrs Handwick had hoped I would be. But I enjoyed Andrea's piano playing, especially as she got more advanced. The measured musical sounds accompanied my sorting of Meccano pieces. Even the scales pleased me, because I could predict the sound that would come next.

'It's a shame we can't play duets,' Andrea said.

There was one important thing Andrea and I had in common. Stories. The Handwick's library was, of course, full of books. Two desks stood back-to-back, and a wooden reading surface ran along the far side of the wall. A cosy niche, set with a cushioned seat for two, suited us perfectly as we shared one book after another. We quite liked the encyclopaedia that had open-out diagrams in the back, especially the one of the full length frog displaying its internal organs.

There was a pair of white gloves sitting ready on the notebook box, in case someone opened one of the precious volumes. These were denied us unless an adult was present. Mostly these were aged tomes that wouldn't have interested us, but one of them did. We grew to cherish it.

Mr Handwick was not always at home when I visited, but I remember him particularly in the library. His broad shoulders filled the doorway and when he turned, he often had a stack of new books in his hands, some of them for us. He'd grin and make us pull one out of the pile with our eyes shut. The one we chose we had to read aloud. They were all just right for our age, so the one we selected never left us panicking about too-difficult words.

At bedtime, Mrs Handwick gathered us up into blanketed bundles and let us snuggle into the revolving leather chairs either side of the biggest study desk. She would take the static Captain's chair and ask, 'What will it be, then, children?'

We would look at each other and smile. We had one absolute favourite book. If we cheated and asked for a different story, it would only be so our wondrous story could be told last.

On the top shelf, with cream cartridge covers and an elegant title in delicate italic script, was a story that we could never hear often enough. Mrs Handwick slipped on her white gloves and stood tall to reach down *Tiressica, The Swans' Journey.*

The story began with a little girl who lived in a long, thin house just like Andrea's, but this one backed onto the river. Every day she would sit on the back wall and wait until the swans sailed by. Then she would feed them with the scraps she had saved. She was a lonely little girl who was unhappy at home. The swans were her friends; they would eat from her hand.

One day something frightening happened in the tall, thin house and the girl cowered by the back wall, hiding. A large figure could just be seen, mostly by shadow, coming out of the back door. Rapidly the first swan lifted its strong neck and the girl clambered on. Then the swan swam off magnificently, leaving its mates to hiss and spread their wings threateningly towards the hovering shadow. Away the first swan sailed, the girl on its back, down river and along river until a large cloud seemed to block its path. But the swan ducked its head and broke through to show the girl a wondrous land beyond, called Tiressica.

I have a vision of white castles and utter happiness ever more, but I can't remember the story detail. I only remember hearing the story, night after night, during my stays at the Handwicks followed by our re-enactments, Andrea trembling on a chair. I, the main swan, knelt down to let her climb on my back before we sailed away to safety. It felt magical, and always left me with a deep sense of calm and goodwill. I had saved the girl, even if I hadn't been able to save my parents.

Years later, lonely in my university student bedroom, I'd recall those times. They would give me comfort.

Whether it was Mr Handwick's influence or my uncle's, I can't say, but after university I landed in this firm and—given I had few distractions - with application, I rose up its ladder rapidly. The work scene became the whole of my daily life. I didn't bother contacting university friends.

As soon as I got my own flat, Aunt and Uncle became distant memories and when Andrea went to Nottingham University, I lost contact with the Handwicks, too.

It wasn't many years before I was given this large office we're sitting in today, together with responsibility for many company employees. It was easy enough to absorb myself completely in my rôle and the needs of the firm. I've been here ever since, a very comfortable couple of decades.

Let me think. It must have been a week after I'd refused that young woman permission to attend her aunt's funeral that I saw a photograph of Mr Handwick in the newspaper on my desk. I knew him at once, although he had aged. The report was about his dramatic death. He happened, by chance, to step into the path of armed robbers escaping from a raid in Oxford Street. This drama shook me to the core. It was even more shocking to see his address. Pledd Close retirement flats, Walthamstow.

I rang the Handwicks' old house immediately, but the female answering said she had lived there for nine years. The previous owner had been a lady on her own with many sub-tenants. When I pressed her, she disclosed this was a Mrs Handwick who provided rooms with bed and breakfast.

If only I had kept in touch! After all Mrs Handwick had done for me, I could have helped, maybe even financially. For her to have been reduced to running such an establishment, presumably carving up the rooms to make umpteen bedrooms - how foul! And Andrea, Andrea—where was she? Where could she be? I put two of my newcomers on the job of research, indicating Brownie points might well be gained.

Andrea. Her address pinned down, Brownie points awarded, a telephone number eventually followed and I picked up the phone, wondering at myself. How could something, someone so special, all that family, so kind, so important in my past, just slip away, be *allowed* to slip away, merely by virtue of "other things": university life, exams, job interview, career, flat-finding, colleagues, meetings, job responsibilities?

Andrea was pleased to hear from me; I could hear warmth in her voice. She was in dreadful shock over her father's sudden death, and busy with funeral arrangements, various problems. I gently queried his address. Pledd Close, Walthamstow! Yes, Daddy had lost his job and couldn't get another before he retired. Her parents had divorced over the financial stress. Daddy had been on the fated Lloyds list. Mummy had needed to sell the house contents and, despite all her Bed and Breakfast efforts, eventually she had sold the house. She now lived at Broadstairs with her sister. And how was I?

I was glad to help over practicalities and to be their support at the funeral, though it made me very sad to see gaunt Mrs Handwick who retained none of her old aplomb, not a trace. It had never occurred to me times might change and someone might need me to help them, as they had helped me. And now it seemed too late to make significant improvements.

As for Andrea, the shiny hair now looped either side of her teary face; the pianist's hands, those long fingers that had glued the fabric clips to the dolls' house people; the slim ankles that had raced me round the many rooms of their house, I'd missed her.

Somewhere deep inside me, I'd been missing all of them, and not been aware of it.

Andrea murmured, 'I have nothing left, you know. The entire contents were sold, every stick of furniture, every picture, every book.' (*Every* book? I dared not ask). 'I was already living at my flat, so luckily I didn't see everything go. But it must have been ghastly for Mummy.'

The lovely contents of all those rooms! The piano, the billiards table, the playroom, the log fire, the niche in the library, Mr Handwick's broad shoulders. The stacks of books. Even the white gloves. It didn't bear thinking about.

Afterwards, not at the funeral gathering, but two days later - a drive away, for 'a breath of fresh air' - I took Andrea to Tintern. It wasn't crowded, not even at the abbey itself. As always, we liked different things. I was soon tired of the empty ruin; she wanted to wander in and out, reading the information, examining the stones themselves, probably imagining the building as it had been, whole.

I left her to it, saying I would stroll up the main road and collect her later. I'd take her for lunch in the next pull-in where there were gift shops and a little art gallery.

I made my way up the main road, stopping when I saw a second-hand bookshop on the other side. *Stella and Rose*, rare and out-of-print books. I wandered in and found room after room, the bookcases clearly labelled, all the books carefully categorised, some of them valuable. It was a paradise of reading. I was at risk of being there all day, especially when I found the middle room upstairs had the best view over Tintern.

The clock struck, I hurried downstairs. Andrea would have finished at the abbey by now. Leaving the bookshop was a wrench, but I could bring her here after lunch. She'd love it.

As I moved to the door, the shelf of antique children's books caught my eye and it was there, *The Swans' Journey!* I knew from the spine it had to be the same one, even though I couldn't remember its full title. The shop-keeper got it down for me. *Tiressica!* I bought it before she could decide to hang onto it. I didn't even ask the price. As soon as it was safely bagged, I thanked her elaborately. Such precious finds she caretakes; their discovery must bring such joy.

'I'll come back,' I told her, 'with my friend, after lunch.' I hurried off, carrying the only thing that could be salvaged for Andrea. It might warm her poor heart.

From the Avon's left bank, the water lit the abbey ruins, the grey-white stone like lace in the pale sun. I was far enough away not to see any coaches, near enough to appreciate its beauty. The strong yet delicate structure stood empty, tantalizingly penetrable, a body with its heart extracted.

Ha! A sudden pain in my chest. I press it and slow my pace, but it is only a thought. *Only?* No, a realisation; so so late in the day, so delayed. That bookshop, perhaps all bookshops, they are my *Tiressica*. That illustration I'd not been able to recall was the swan with its saved girl breaching the mist into secret safety.

Did my heart stop at my mother's words, 'Shall I buy him a little book?' and has it only now started again? At least I can feel it beat. How curious!

Andrea is coming towards me. I have something important for her, held against my heart.

A HIPPOPOTAMUS IS BECOMING

His feet turn outwards and his walk is disjointed.

After I've followed him to the end of the last paved road, I've worked out what's so odd about this. My steps have a rhythm to them, his do not. It reminds me of the first time I heard a melody in five-four time. I had to listen several times to work out the initially confusing pattern.

His *one-two, one-two-three, one, one,* steps falter a moment as he checks his bag, apparently for a lunch snack. But no, the plastic bag he pulls out contains slices of water melon, lettuce and alfafa. He checks them, nods to himself, and strides on, jerkily but purposefully. It doesn't seem as if he's heading for the social club. I speed ahead and introduce myself, in case he's heard of my arrival. He hasn't. But he does open a conversation.

'No advance warning of your arrival. But welcome. Adrian Le Bow. Perhaps you'll be glad to know that in the future.'

'Sure, Adrian. I've been looking forward to meeting people. You're the first. Do you know everyone?'

He turns his head and meets my eyes for the first time. 'Perhaps. "You must socialise," they advised me, "as soon as you arrive. The Limpopo community are a lively lot. Put yourself around." So I did.'

'And was that successful?'

'There is a swimming club. I dislike swimming. The social club is for inveterate drinkers. I am not. Is that you? No? Then regard your posting as a temporary discomfort. You must try to adapt.'

I ask if he's managed to do so.

'Ah.' He motions to a large log, and we sit down, side-by-side, swatting the flies and shying away from stray mangy dogs that linger. 'Disappointingly, the Limpopo Philately Club have few female enthusiasts. As a contender for social excitement, it has failed me completely. I have tried venues for tea and venues for alcohol: neither have yielded ladies who latch.'

I nod sympathetically.

'And, my one "match" proving to be frigid, the Singles Social Society have lost a male member. I've moved on. Our nearest water-hole reserve enjoys my attentions now.'

'Really?'

'Indeed. I've introduced myself in gentle stages, waited discreetly to be noticed and then claimed. This has paid off. I'm accepted now. I've learned which customs are crucial. I am getting success. So gratifying that Lavinia is spending less time submerged.'

'Submerged!'

His eyes, green under untended eyebrows, seek mine, as if seeking a matching enthusiasm. He waves towards the water reserve where the hippopotamus is reported to rule. Has he attached to one?

'I approach, wearing waders and a rubber suit looking more like her than me, a gesture Lavinia appreciates. She runs forward, so fast for her short legs, clearly eager for contact. I've taught her to observe Health and Safety notices by dribbling them with urine I garner from different sources during the week. Demonstrating compliance has put her ahead of others in the water reserve. Achieving this has substantially improved my confidence.'

'I can imagine.'

'She's clever, you know: not fazed by problem-solving mazes anymore. And she knows the actions for getting rewards: a drooping head gains lettuce.' He indicates his plastic bag. 'She lifts one leg for pumpkin; and for water melon, squats down.'

'Impressive.' What else could I say?

He leans forward. The hippo rewards gleam stickily in the unfriendly sun. 'She's started to eat alfafa from my hand, although she prefers it on mud. I join her there, slithering and sliding in the bank's black liquid. Lavinia nudges me up with her snout. Her nostrils are enormous. I think of them as channels to her brain.

'We communicate through sounds: note, tone, length and source. She's culturally responsive. I bring my iPod here sometimes. She received *The Messiah* more enthusiastically than Madonna.'

'How do you know?'

'Her explosive utterances testified to it.'

'Only music, or the human voice?'

He nods, closing his eyes a moment. 'A megaphone works well for stimulating her literary awareness. When Lavinia casts me an expectant glance, I read, tenor-toned. We've covered poetry, but not yet narrative verse. I think *Paradise Lost* will appeal. I'm convinced she'll compose a rejoinder, and then I'll read her *Paradise Regained*.'

'Goodness!' I mop the back of my neck with my already damp handkerchief.

'It's taken time, but these days she'll peer straight into my eyes. She holds my gaze, clearly sensing my mood, either rubbing her flank against my solar plexus or gaping to show me her uvula. The cloud of her appalling breath envelops my emerging emotions.'

His tenor becomes mezzo-soprano as his words speed on.

'You see, it's Lavinia who's taught me about feelings. *Humour*: when I'm static, stuck in mud to my thighs, she winks with her wondrous eyelashes; *irritation*: if I sneeze, she'll tail-flick flies at me; *jealousy*: if I attend to food she butts me, tramples my sandwich into the mud and rolls on it, legs aloft; and *loyalty*: she expresses total submission by spraying me with faeces. Should I visit a day late, she'll stomp up to me, turn her back and fart. That's *love!*'

I recoil. I'm regretting my posting to Limpopo. Let there be others whose pleasures are nearer my own! I stand, 'I must try to—'

'Lavinia! *Lavinia Le Bow* runs off the tongue so beautifully. She deserves a full name in appreciation of what she's become, or becoming. A hippopotamus is becoming my closest friend.'

He grabs his bag of rewards, and raises a hand. 'Lavinia's waiting.' He leaves me, leaning into his unstable stride as the track takes him downhill and towards increasingly wild and muddy terrain.

TRUTH THERAPY

'I can't stop telling lies.'

My new client strides into my consulting room and makes himself comfortable, almost before I've given my usual introductory phrases. Those are intended to reassure.

Perhaps he needs no reassurance. He's an attractive man, sandy-haired, freckled, high cheek bones, well-toned body. Leaning forward, his arm on his knee to support his head, he portrays the word that might sum him up, *Sincerity.*

'Aidan, isn't it? Why do I do it?' He bangs his forehead as if anguished. And since there can be no answer from someone he's only just met, however well qualified, he pushes his head forward to me. 'I just lie the whole time.'

'It's almost as if you're lying now.'

He starts, rises a touch from his chair. 'You're so right. This is why I came to you, instead of…' He looks abashed.

I am aware he went to the other clinic first.

'… I didn't actually *go* to Abbey Consultants. Donna made the appointment for me, but at Reception I turned away. I walked around for the hour and then went home. I lied to her about going.'

'You lied about going.'

'Yes. You see, I felt I couldn't be wholly frank with a woman counsellor, and I'd be too embarrassed to tell all this to another man.' He blushes, 'But with you being g—' he looks at the floor, '—not so macho, I feel I can probably tell you.'

'So you felt able to make this appointment.'

There's a pause. 'Actually, when Donna found out I hadn't been to Abbey, *she* made it. But *I* found you, I chose you from the photos in the leaflets. She said, "All right, I don't mind which one you go to, but just go." She came with me, and I expect she's waiting outside now to know I have actually attended this appointment.'

'And that helps?'

'Well I won't have to lie about it, will I?'

'So—'

He laughs. 'Like, doing what I'm told makes me tell the truth.'

There's a long pause. I look at him, expectant.

He gives way, pushes his lips forward. 'Why does Donna want me to come here, you're thinking? It's only about the lies. My lying. We have the perfect relationship. My lies are the only thing that's wrong.'

'The only thing wrong between yourself and your—wife, is it?'

'Yes, wife. I'm so lucky. My wife is everything a man could want: caring, brilliant cook, attractive, successful, good manager, clever in the house, big b–', he cups his hands, 'sexy. I should respect her, I DO respect her but when I lie, she sees that as disrespectful.'

'Do you agree?'

'Not really.'

'Is it only your wife you lie to.'

He thinks. 'Well, no.'

'Perhaps it would help if you told me the times or occasions when you lie.'

'I lie *all the time*. I tell myself not to, but I just can't help it.' He looks at me helplessly.

'It's as though it's not your fault.'

'Exactly.' He sits back, looking relieved. 'I knew you'd sort it, somehow.'

'No. We're here to work on a way for *you* to sort it.'

'With your help, your guidance.'

'Like it's my responsibility.'

'No, no of course not. I mean, it must be my responsibility, mustn't it? They're my lies.'

'Yes. They're yours. Tell me about the lies.'

'Where do I start?' He spreads his hands. 'It's happening all the time.'

'Like the weather?'

'Ha! Like the weather! It comes and does its stuff all day, every day.'

'Yesterday?'

'The sort of things that happen? Yesterday. I'd had a shitty day. Well, most days at the office are shitty. I'm a loss adjustor. People's stories - you wouldn't believe!'

His face brightens, his eyes widen. He's about to give me anecdotes but stops himself. That's encouraging. I don't move a muscle.

'Mustn't go into that, must think of yesterday, what happened. I came home, went into the kitchen, Donna wasn't there, a bit late. If I'm first home, it would be reasonable for me to empty the dishwasher, the clothes dryer, that sort of thing.'

He stops at that point and appears to forget me. I notice a slight flush beginning at the bottom of his neck.

'But...?' There's no answering movement. I prompt again with, 'What happened after you went into the kitchen?'

He jerks upright, smiles, glances at me. 'I picked up the morning's paper from the island and read a bit about a bloke who'd had something removed from his—'

He snorts, but again I avoid moving.

'I was reading, and then heard the key in the front door. I had the dishwasher open before she got to the kitchen, and two plates in my hand when she said, "Hello darling, I'm sorry, management meeting's put me right behind. I haven't picked up the shopping, totally bushed, I can't cook tonight. Can you go for a Chinese? Not the nearest one. Their pak choy is always soggy, the further one. Get chicken with lemon, and vegetable side dish."

'I put the plates down, pulled my jacket back on. Patted my pocket for my wallet.

"Oh," she says, quite nicely, "you haven't unpacked the dishwasher yet? How long have you been in?"

"Just this minute."

"But you've been reading the newspaper."

"No. Haven't a clue what's in it."

'See, Aidan, first lie.'

I nod. 'I noticed.'

'Yes. I say quickly, "I was starting to unpack the dishes." I point to the plates as evidence. "Hungry, better go for the Chinese." And I slip out quickly. Go to the Chinese, the first one actually. It's much nearer, and I'm tired. Also, the pub's next door. I put in the order and ask them to go easy with the pak choy. Pop in for a beer. Just one.'

A pause. I keep my face expressionless, but my eyes in his direction.

He looks at me. 'Well two, in fact. I'm going to be straight with you. It was two. Then I pick up the order, and trot home. Donna's unpacked the dishwasher, laid the table, opened the wine, changed out of her In-Your-Face dress and glossy tights, into her leopard onesie with the top-to-toe zip. She's finished the paper, it's folded up, immaculate, ready for the recycle, or even me, if I have time to read it. She's already put the recycling tubs for metal and glass at the back door. She says, "Hooray, you're back. I'm starving. I had to work through lunch, again."

"Not fair, darling."

"My responsibility. As Senior Operations Manager, I'm needed everywhere." She's already spooning the rice onto our plates. "Why were you so long?"

"Long? Was I? I came straight home."

"You were ages. When I go, I've found they serve really quickly. What happened?"

'I look busy with the plastic container of vegetables, hooking the pak choy to the top so it's less swamped by the juices.

"Dean?"

'I have to answer then. "You wanted me to go to the further one. It's a long long walk to Peking Heaven."

"Worth it, though." Spoons out the chicken. "Let's eat."

'I pour the wine. She's inspecting the vegetables. She starts eating. *"This isn't as good as usual."*

'Whoops! So I say quickly, *"Someone in the queue said it was going downhill."*

'There you see, another lie. Complete fabrication.'

I nod. He looks self-satisfied. I test him, 'How do you feel about that?'

'Absolutely wretched! But I don't stop! It goes on from there, one lie after another. And because I feel bad, I tell her I'll do the dishes. She's grateful, flops out on the chaise longue and puts the furry feet of her onesie on the cabriole table I've placed there for her. *"You're a dear,"* she says. *"I've totally had it for today."*

I take the dishes into the kitchen, stack the dishwasher, but she likes the glasses washed up separately. I'm clumsy, one clinks against the sink and the top shatters. She loves those glasses. Her aunty gave us them.

"What's happened?" she calls out.

"Nothing. Just clearing up." I grab another glass from the cupboard and put it on the drainer as if it's just washed, pull the rest of the glasses in the cupboard forward, so the gap doesn't show. I throw the cracked one into the bin but, shit, she's obviously emptied it while I was out so she's bound to see the glass. I unfold the newspaper, tear a sheet off, screw it up tightly and put it over the broken glass, fold the newspaper again with the torn side down-most; wash up the second glass, really carefully. But there are fragments of the first blocking the plughole. I extract them. They're tiny, one sticks into the pad of my finger, it bleeds. I tear a piece of kitchen towel, dab my finger, screw the glass fragments into the piece of kitchen towel, put it in the bin under the newspaper. It's no good. She'll lift the newspaper out to recycle it, and then she'll see what's underneath. Best I take the bin liner outside to the rubbish bin and shove the contents down hard. Then it'll be hidden by the mess. I open the back door ready.

"What are you doing?"

"Taking out the rubbish."

"*Done it!*" she says, but I close the door so she'll think I haven't heard.

'I come back, put on a new bin liner trying to do it so quietly she won't hear. Then I go into her, ready for our cosy evening. I lean over her prone body, all furry in its onesie, and kiss the only bare part of her, her forehead. She has a stapled sheaf of papers on her stomach. "*Look!*" she says triumphantly, holding it out to me. "*That report I've been agonizing over. Have a read. It's done. Kelsie managed to proof and print it out for me before I left the office. I've got to present it to the share-holders tomorrow. I hope they're going to be impressed.*"

"*I'm certain they will be,*" I say, taking the report. A smear of blood decorates the title page.

"*Oh no! God!*" she says. "*It's marked. I can't present it like this!*"

"*Shit! So, so, sorry!*" I put the report down hurriedly. "*What shall I do, wipe it down with a bacterial wipe?*"

Then she says, "*That won't come off. It's blood! You've cut your finger. How did you do that?*"

"*Nothing. I think it was something sharp caught on my jacket. I didn't take much notice at the time.*"

We both look doubtfully at the neat spot of blood on my finger.

"*Pass me the phone,*" she says, pressing a contact key. "*Kelsie! Sorry to wreck your evening. Emergency. My husband's put a bloody finger on my title page. Can you re-print it? We're in the board room at 9.30 sharp. Yes, sod's law. You're brill. Thanks.*" She hands me back the phone. "*What a treasure! Works all hours, hoping for promotion. Shall we watch something?*"

'I nod, grateful.

"*Bargain Hunt?*"

I hate Bargain Hunt. "*Yes, let's,*" I say, finding the channel.

"*But I'm not sure you really like that.*"

"*Darling, I love it,*" I say.

'You see, another lie. But in my position, wouldn't anyone have lied?' He sits forward, *Sincerity* again, holds out his hands, palms up, beams. 'There! I've given you a whole evening of lies!'

'It's almost as if I was there,' I say, noting the end of the performance.

'So, what do I do, where do I go from here, now I've told you the whole truth?'

'Whole? One evening.'

He sits back, abashed. 'Yes, but it's the sort of thing. Now you can see—.' A pause, waiting for me to come out with all the answers.

Pause failing, he goes on, 'In your job, what sort of thing do you do now, to cure, to put things right?'

'What do you think should happen?'

'I should stop lying.'

I wait.

'But that's why I've come to you. For help to stop.'

'Perhaps we need to look at causes.'

'Why I do it? Yes. Why?,' he bangs his forehead. '*Why?* There's just no excuse.' He pulls at his shirt. 'See this? Lovely shirt, chosen by Donna, bought by Donna, washed and ironed by Donna. She couldn't be more caring, more loving. Even this - this *lying*, she's so understanding. She just says she's sad I do it, wants to help me to stop. She had the idea of counselling, found the clinics.'

'Yes. She had the idea.'

'So—?'

'Did you both want you to stop lying?"

'Oh, of course!' A slight shake of the head. 'Of *course*. I mean it's terrible. A man in my situation, just lying and lying.'

'You don't see any reason for it?'

He shakes his head, mystified expression.

'Perhaps if you shut your eyes…'

He shuts them as fast as if I've shouted a command.

'Try this. There's nothing in this room except my chair and yours and the space in between. Explore that space, if you like, with your eyes closed.'

He stands, hands out in front of him, walks around slowly, a smile on his face. 'I can't see a thing, Aidan. I wonder, if I shut my eyes before I speak, whether I could tell the truth.'

'I wonder.'

'Should I try?'

'Should you? How are you feeling now?'

'Good. This feels good.'

He's turning this way and that, exploring, a few steps forward, sidesteps, a few back again. He waves his outstretched arms, hands splayed.

I encourage him. 'Is there anything you'd like to say? Shout perhaps? The consulting room is sound-proofed.'

'Really?'

'Really. No-one can hear except me.'

'Hell!' he says, a little louder than usual. 'Leave off!' Louder still. He kicks one foot forward. 'Leave me alone. Shove off. You're a bitch!' He punches the air, once, twice. His colour rises. 'Yes. Fucking bitch. I'd like to tear your appraisal sheets into shreds...' He twists around as though scattering fragments to the winds. He screws his eyes tight, spreads his legs and his chest as he stands tall. 'I'd like to spray all your bloody reports with semen,' His words start firing from his mouth at a tremendous rate, 'bite your buttocks, butt my head on your breasts, shovel them into my wet mouth, beat off your brawny biceps, run my bared teeth hard down your arm.' His knees are bent, he's leaning forward. 'No more of you on top! I'll pin you down, no, I'll stand back, take a running leap at your body and press my weight down so hard we fall through the mattress and rut on the carpet till you're screaming to stop.'

The word "stop" seems to slow him. He stands straight again, shakes a stiff finger left to right. 'You'll fight me off, but I shall win.' Tosses his head, 'I don't care what you think, I want WAR, not love.' His face and neck are dark crimson. He blinks. 'Have I done it? Shall I stop?'

'When you wish.'

He opens his eyes slowly, reaches to his handkerchief, beautifully pressed, and wipes his mouth. He sits down. When I see him scanning my face, I spread my hands wide. 'How are you feeling?'

'Released,' he says. 'Wow!' The dark red begins to fade from his cheeks. 'So...'

'Deep breath. So, Dean. Now you have a lot to think about.' I look at the clock. 'And we must stop there.'

'No.'

'Fifty minutes. Time's up. It's important we keep to our boundaries.'

'But what now…?'

'I suggest you go home and quietly reflect on what's just happened. Let me know your thoughts when you come next. Same time next week?' I stand up.

'Ah.' He looks around, spots my back door behind the curtain. 'I'll pop out this way. Could you tell Donna I've already gone? I'd rather cool down before facing her. She's bound to ask what I said, you see. Just tell her I'm not here.'

'But you are here. You want me to pretend you're not!'

'Yes please. I can slip out now, so by the time you get to reception, it won't be a lie.'

'Mine or yours?'

HARRIET INTERVENES

I'm Harriet, female, so not legitimate in this book, but I want to seriously suggest more appealing male examples should put themselves forward on dating sites. You've just read how dreadfully Donna's match turned out. Dean! How disastrous a marriage that's going to be.

A dating site is supposed to match you with a male who suits. I wouldn't expect it to offer up a curious man for a date, let alone more than one. You're about to learn I wasn't served well in my own recent event. I think you need to know what led to my encounter.

When you met me in Me-time Tales, I'd been matched and was in love with Matt; ultimately, less with the man than the mattress he bought me when we parted. I could hardly bring myself to move off it.

Blissfully relaxed every night (and much of the day) on my mattress, I didn't expect much to change. Then horror! Strange red patches appeared all over my legs. And they itched so. Scratch, scratch, nothing helped. Now I just had to get out of bed and dash to the Health Centre.

On the way, this colourful advert for Speedy Dating took my eye. I was thinking how impossible dating would be now, while I displayed the irritating rash to the practice nurse. But the shock of learning the cause was worse than the itching.

Bed bugs! Yes! Apparently, they're rife this year because of the lengthy heatwave. The nurse assured me the lotion would work quite rapidly.

Pacing home via the pharmacy, I had one target in mind and it wasn't a man. It was the bed.

I man-handled it furiously, turned its far side upward and—oh, my goodness, the nurse was right. The horrible things were crawling about underneath my beautiful mattress. If only I hadn't spent such a time lying on it! It was a love affair with that mattress; memory foam that remembers every crease and undulation of my body, an attention no-one had paid it before. And now it had betrayed me by harbouring a vile enemy. Could Matt have deliberately infected it—a punishment for ending our relationship?

My vacuum cleaner is reliably vicious. I grabbed its hose and applied its aperture to every millimetre of my bed and bedroom. The nurse advised that the beastly bedbugs slide in under the door, so I went on a killing spree from bedroom to hallway, bathroom, living room, entrance, and even the windowsills. Then I worried about my vacuum being full of bedbugs surviving, even multiplying, in the warm environment of a vacuum bag. I chose the powder that's meant for moths, and the powder that's meant for ants, and emptied the entire contents of both into the vacuum bag, shook it up for peace of mind (mine) and hopefully, end of peace (them) and left the bag outside by the bin.

I showered, checked my bathroom floor, the cupboards, the towels, then showered again to be certain. I took care dressing, and because it was so long since I'd bothered to dress properly (mattress life having reigned supreme) I dressed with especial care and attention. Wasn't I worth it? That colourful ad must have been lingering in my consciousness, because I chose my clothes to match each other, and I even applied make-up.

I was now a clean, bug-free person in a bug-free environment, a woman who had left her mattress behind. It would need a daily beating to ensure it hadn't absorbed any bugs into its impressive memory. I would think of Matt as I bashed it.

There must be other men, and speed dating would allow rapid culling of impossible mates. By the time one of them arranged a date with me, the rash would be cured.

My thrilling venue in mind, I left home in a positive mood. Who, or how many who's would I meet?

DATE AT SPEED, HATE AT LEISURE

SPEED DATING. The sign was outlined by two rows of coloured lights curved over the door: one green, one red. If this represented Go and Stop, Stop and Go might be wiser for dating.

Inside, on an Identification label, I wrote, *Harriet*, in the most alluring script I could manage. A few giggles and nervous coughs sounded as The Green and Red lights beamed down on would-be maters. What kind of man might suggest *Green* for me? I didn't consider health preoccupations; only eye colour, voice timbre, occupation, stance. Such a mistake.

The evening whirled by in a confusingly rapid musical chairs during which I hardly managed to offer more than my age to most daters. They were too keen on listing their various achievements and preferences, to which I could only nod before it was time to shunt sideways to face the next prospect. The experience resembled the sushi circle Matt had taken me to at Paddington station before the mattress era: grab quickly, or you miss the most desirable dish.

When the evening ended, the organisers asked us to state our first and second choices. I dithered, trying to remember the fast-moving array of dark, fair, unshaven, bearded, grinning, gawping line-up of potential dates. Had I a preference? Perhaps the one with a ginger beard? But it was too late. The square-shouldered man (symmetrical features) who selected me, unequivocally, was announcing himself as Rowan Blay-Hiscoby.

How can I describe him? His eyes were light brown and focussed, he paid attention to what he was saying, he didn't look around at other people, his shirt collar was striped and loose and his feet narrow with tightly knotted laces. He was taller than me, though his legs didn't seem to straighten fully when he stood still. His hair was neat and brownish and he'd titivated it with gel. I didn't notice any smell; I mean like Diesel, Joop or bad breath. He looked more or less the same age as me, but he explained he'd gone into business rather than undertake a university course, and now worked part-time "Necessarily". I decided not to follow that up, although this was obviously his intention. I don't like doing what is expected.

He asked for a date. Me, a date! After all this time, Mattless.

We went to Margate in his car. And sat on a bench looking at the sea.

He began the conversation. 'You enjoy music?'

'I do. I play the flute.'

He breathed out, eyes closed, nostrils flared as I chatted on, musically.

Rowan led me on a walk, hand-in-hand on the sand. We passed a seaweed circle with a poorly spelled message conveyed in stones, *A good Musim is a ded one.* I peeped sideways to gauge his reaction; holding similar attitudes is important. His mind was on higher things.

'Best stay walking on a flat level. I'm against undue exertion,' he stated, gesturing to the gently sloping bank behind us, where a cheery fox terrier and a strategically placed office chair defied gravity. 'And I'm allergic to dogs; to most animals, in fact.'

I decided not to mention my little crew: Daisy Anne, a Scottish Fold, snow white with queer little ears - so cute, and not cheap; the guinea pigs, and Caspar, the blue-tongued skink. Bless him, however long I stand and hold Caspar, he remains patient. He'll always hang out with me.

So. My new date wasn't concerned about racist messages or prone to finding the humorous side of Life, and we didn't have animal love in common. We didn't match each other's walking capacity either. But I wanted to give Rowan Blay-Hiscoby every chance to display our suitability as a pair, given he had chosen me from an array of sixteen females.

Our first date ended with his asking me to drive him home. Was it a test? I did my best, but as we reached base, I saw he had his eyes closed, so he'd missed any driving skills I displayed. He said, 'I'm grateful. You can understand I get easily exhausted.'

We'd only walked a few hundred yards and chatted on a bench.

Nevertheless, we ventured out a second time. Still to Margate, perhaps his favourite place. In Herbie's Health Food Restaurant, I chose carefully, but Rowan re-worded my order for Duck Egg Mousse with a knowing smile to the waiter. 'She means Bladderwrack Syllabub, and make that two, please.'

Food differences, I thought. Having the same eating preferences wasn't vital. Most menus offer a choice. It's conversation and shared interests that make a relationship work. I ate obediently, although regretting the lost opportunity to sample Duck Egg Mousse. The wine was fine. Why should I worry? This man was showing a keenness to spend time with me. There was time and opportunity for improvements to pop up, wasn't there?

As our main course disappeared from our plates into our stomachs, Rowan stated, 'A priority in a relationship is that both partners demonstrate their knowledge, talents and skills.' He then demonstrated his - haematology - at length.

I sat back, leaving my knife and fork beautifully aligned on my empty plate. How else could I convey respect?

He continued, 'And yours are?'

I described mine tentatively. 'Music. Reading. Tap dancing.' These seemed trivial, or even unworthy.

Rowan's light eyes scanned my face, or was it the extent of my knowledge, talents and skills? He didn't ask me to elaborate.

The meal wore on. Outside, the evening wore on. I felt worn, like a coat or a cardigan grown shabby. Had he worn me out just as I had worn out the mattress? What with—his interest? Was he too ardent?

No, it was not his heart Rowan Blay-Hiscopy wore on his sleeve but his hypertension, the silent killer he warned me to regard very seriously. I did. I do, but...

After the meal, we walked along the promenade, iridescent from the pier's prisms of light. Margate's so self-aware since its Arts-Council-funded gallery opened, the local shops developing niche window-displays to attract the newly up-marketed residents. I was hovering outside a display of Mannerly Prwyx's textured nose flutes when Rowan pressed my arm and told me he had something important to convey.

It was surely too early in our friendship to commit, but I turned with a suitably softened expression towards my lover-to-be. 'Harriet,' he breathed on an impressive tenor note, 'you must know something about me.'

'No. Nothing.'

'I mean, I *need* you to know this about me... I am shortly to have a colonoscopy.'

That wasn't what I'd expected to hear. I dropped my hands from my sides and shoved them into my pockets. This wasn't the right moment to demonstrate how well I could tap dance, an idea prompted by Rowan's emphasis on valuing skills. 'Oh dear,' I said. 'An oscopy sounds a touch surgical.'

'More than a touch, Harriet. The specialist will insert a four-foot long, flexible tube about the thickness of a finger into my anus and advance it slowly into my rectum and through the colon as far as the cecum.'

That wasn't funny. 'Oh. Goodness.'

'I shall be hospitalised, of course.'

I turned back to consider the nose flutes. Strange I was focussing upon an aperture at one end of a human while Rowan concentrated on the other end. Was this difference significant or complementary?

'I think you'd be the ideal person to provide me with company and perhaps music while I recuperate. I love that you are musical.'

Turning away while I prepared a suitable answer, I read the caption from the window display. 'In times of mourning or sadness, the twin-pipe nose flute was the perfect conduit for expressing sorrow.' I could buy one for Rowan when I visited him in hospital. After which, he could teach himself the nose flute while recuperating.

We did not have a third date. Rowan Blay-Hiscoby couldn't hold Miss Harriet in a relationship longer than a snake takes to slough its skin.

I suggested his health came first. It was far more important than me.

Our relationship ended after I'd squeezed Rowan's hand and left him to his second injection.

Outside, I conveyed my horrified sympathy to the nurse who advised me the procedures he was undergoing were completely voluntary and investigative. He'd booked himself in for private treatment including "recovery" and insisted upon a full anaesthetic. Other people just have a local, and make their own way home after the examination. I would have given him a lift.

A thought. If my mattress can be fumigated, I can use it again.

Speed dating is for discovering a soul you can mate with. I felt safer mateless. And for Rowan Blay Hiscoby, I was a disappointment. He might get luckier in Outpatients.

SEEN FROM THE COACH

The millennium has long passed. Against the warnings and predictions, we are all still here. And, increasingly, more and more of us are here. Lots of us. That's what I'm noticing. And something happened recently that made me think more about the fact.

I no longer drive. Outings, holidays, I make them by public transport. I take a book. Or several. Yesterday, with a copy of Elementary Statistics, I stayed in and read. Studying a new subject averts dementia.

Today I was off to Birkenhead. I'd planned to visit the Wirral Transport Museum & Heritage Tramway by ferry, over the first tramlines to be built, I believe. Now with the coach cancelled, there'll be hours to wait and I've managed to leave my book behind. That means sitting here, thinking. I'd be glad of someone to talk to. There's something on my mind I'd like to discuss. It troubles me. I think I should have taken some action, but it's too late now.

It's the last trip that's preoccupying me. France—not the tramping around cathedrals and vineyards, but what I saw during the return journey. It haunts me.

This particular trip, I managed to finish *Uncle Tom's Cabin*, a book I started at school and found too taxing, but vowed I'd read properly one day. And that day came on the France trip. By the fourth day, such a long day, I finished the book. A sad, sad tale. What terrible beings we humans are! If only I hadn't looked out of the window to divert my thoughts from those distressing events, I wouldn't have witnessed another.

I was peering through the dark, mindlessly. Imagine it. Let me take you there...

The coach is full downstairs. Upstairs, I'm one of six passengers, the only one awake. The commentary's completed, the tour is over bar the homeward run.

We've left the chalk cliffs behind. We're alongside cornfields in heavy traffic. Surrounding us, six lanes of snarled vehicles.

We drive towards a lay-by, long, and sided by a ditch. The stream of traffic surges ahead but we slow, our travel-sick passenger seeking respite. He alights.

In a country lane beyond a hedge, invisible except for someone high up, stands one ten ton truck, two men: the fat driver, the lean assistant. Two torches play low.

The tailgate opens, sheep baa into the night. Beneath them, sixteen wooden crates creak. The fat and lean men sort sheep, shift them, just the first few.

Then. Sixteen pairs of eyes, near blind, incognito. Sixteen pairs of feet, sixteen soles seeking sanctuary. Thin legs poke out downwards reaching for the muddy ground, a downtrodden ditch. The dark ground receives their staggering descent into nothingness. Limbs unfold, painfully slow. Like stick insects, they slide into the undergrowth. The fat man chucks a package to one side of them, points to the adjoining cornfield beyond which perhaps they'll find some tin construction, their future place of work. A breath of wind helps the corn acknowledge them. Sheaves lean towards their wasted cheeks, their desperate eyes.

The lean assistant unearths a pile of bundles, drops them onto the mud, then he boots the freed sheep up the slope, back onto the tailgate. They hoof it over the crates bumping their woolly sides against each other. The baa-ing quietened, the lean one lopes to his high seat at the front of the lorry. The fat man locks up, rubs his hands on the seat of his pants and spits. He doesn't look into the swaying corn, its new-formed corridors closing behind the creeping figures. Does he compose himself before he abandons his dependents? No. He hoists himself into his king of the road position. The truck drives away to the end of the lay-by.

Our coach remains still. Outside it, oblivious, our sickly passenger pads a path parallel to the drama.

Our driver leans out to call sympathetically, 'Take your time mate, just walk up and down till you feel okay. Tailback anyway, in'it? I'll have a smoke.' He opens his door, strikes a match, his face alight for that first comforting pull.

Downstairs, thirty-nine passengers tut or snore.

Ahead, the truck is waiting to join the traffic jam. Should I alert our driver? Can the truck be intercepted, its driver punished? It's departing, its back end belching smoke. Briefly, its back lights illuminate the last of the skinny limbs escaping from the ditch into the swaying corn, the last glimmer highlighting a hand grasping the clutch of battered bundles. Its cargo lighter, the truck disappears, sucked into three lanes of heavy traffic.

Left in the dark, the sixteen become invisible. Unprotected. Should I say something? Who to? What for—now?

I've watched the event from the warmth of my paid-for padded seat, with my luggage stowed and a coach driver tuned to my needs. I've remained silent. I've done nothing. Useless. Wordless. Worthless.

And now, every time I have no book, I see a cornfield somewhere in England, a darkened lay-by, the glow from our driver's cigarette, the dust from a departed truck, the gold and green of this untroubled land.

LETTING GO

Martin put the phone down after his father's call. Some addled tale of a coach trip; figures crawling through a cornfield in the dark! Poor old Dad. At least coach trips got him out of his retirement flat.

As for himself...

He cradled the bottle of brandy. It had been a disastrous day; one that ridiculed his perversity in lurching through the hoops of the last two decades: school, exams, training, selection, work, promotion, dating, marriage, divorce.

Misery had begun with school: memorizing times tables, covering books, losing them, detentions, school holidays wrecked by writing about them, tests, grading, red pen, preparing—joy (for the parents) about his grammar school place, misery—for him. What did it offer, that daunting building: the long walk to it, damp blazer, muddy shoes, failing radiators, jostling in the corridors, evenings hunched over textbooks with their spiteful fonts.

Meanwhile, the fond parents, ensured of Martin's education, relaxed with TV and a crackling fire. Exams blighted his teens. The evenings of preparation caged up, to be condemned to the serried desks for anxious hours of scribbling. Ultimately, the paralyzing boredom of Speech Day preceded the agonising suspense before Results.

At last, an end to school. He wore the new raincoat for his interview not to ruin his only suit. With dread, he approached Thurber Insurance Services, its glass edifice identified throughout his teens as the acme of success. Then his "Achievement" of gaining a post celebrated by his proud parents with a dinner out —chewy steak and even beer. This to mark his gateway to adulthood.

What did this achievement bring, this "wonderful opportunity"? It meant braving the brunt of the office with its gripes and spites and little meannesses; slogging daily by train and tube *to* work, *from* work; twelve years of the open-plan office, each day filled with tension, trouble-avoidance and boredom. At last, angst-filled appraisals led to promotions. Any new rôle was played out against gossip, slightings, rivalries, befriendings and betrayals, the swaggering beside the water dispenser, the constant breathing-down-neck of a senior geek called Gilbert.

More recently, the innovation of management weekends brought humiliations, trials by peer judgement. Martin had survived everything until the last wavering signs of *Making It* were withdrawn.

How miserably he'd failed the "Inspire Greatness" weekend! Younger, cheerier colleagues surpassed him in rushing under ropes and identifying ways to traverse muddy trenches for *Your Team*. He couldn't think of more than three uses of a brick, and he'd gone early to bed after the abseiling. He hadn't realised the evening drinking in the bar was a test of social skills.

On his thankful return to the office, his relief was dashed. A summons to the managers' suite informed him he had "reached his potential" in the firm. His salary would be maintained, but ceilinged. He was invited to move four floors down, together with the contents of his desk.

Younger colleagues sweated there, angling for a position on the floors above. Martin quickly discovered there would be no individual laptop to take home whenever it suited him, no independence, no view from the windows, no sandwich trolley.

He eked out the day in the rear-most of the eight forward-fronting desks. Every time he lifted his eyes from his computer screen, he faced the pustules on his new colleague's neck. In desperation, he made an excuse to check the archives on the twenty-seventh floor, where he made the task as lengthy as possible. On his return to Floor Four he was trapped in the lift with a gloating Gilbert. As Martin pressed the lift button, Gilbert quipped, 'Going down, I see.'

Now he was home, "relaxing" on his squeaky black faux leather sofa, facing photos of the wife who'd got fed up months before. She'd suddenly left both him and the ironing.

What was it for, all that grafting for years? He filled his glass again. It had been a cheat, a lifetime's fraud. Carrie had twigged it; that's why she'd left, for someone more successful. She wouldn't spend any more evenings home alone while Martin slogged in the office in the faint hope of further promotion—for loyalty and hard-work if not for acumen. She had a job of her own —no, a career. She was probably being praised and promoted this very moment. He'd tried to be a powerfully successful husband. It hadn't been worth the effort.

Before the brandy bottle was empty, Martin put the TV on as an excuse for lolling on the sofa. If he hadn't strived as he'd been brought up to do, he wouldn't have progressed to management. If he'd never bothered, never passed an exam, *never sat one*, he'd have manned a small shop, a short walk away. By six p.m. he'd have slumped on the sofa, guiltless, each working day of his adult life. As a non-academic youngster, he'd have joined his parents in the evenings, perhaps laughing at a TV show together or even *going out*. He might have joined the snooker club, and there made unambitious friends he'd still have today.

Martin reviewed the life he hadn't had as an assistant, working a mere nine-to-five day, at the end of which, *End.* No phone calls with queries, no briefcases full of work, no early starts for special assignments, no self-assessment sheets, no returning home late, too shattered for sex. Having fulfilled his responsibilities by five p.m. every evening, he and Carrie could have taken off and enjoyed themselves, instead of devoting their lifestyle to Getting On. He'd been conned.

The door banged. Joe, his one and only, arriving home late after football. His school was nearer here than to Carrie's new place, where he spent the weekends.

Martin summoned up a cheery greeting and replaced the brandy bottle in its closed cupboard. Best not prove Carrie correct in her parting shot, "Leaving you to your drink and your miserable life," as she left for a better life with a better man.

He heard Joe putting a pizza in the microwave. He joined him in the kitchen, leaning on the door jamb, partly for support.

'Hi, Dad. We won. I stopped three goals.'

'Great.' It was good to listen to Joe's roll-back of the game. Listening took no effort.

He watched Joe munch his way through his pizza. 'Have salad with that.' He opened the fridge and put a portion beside Joe.

'Ugh.'

Martin found himself minding a lot about Joe's five-a-day. He kept his hand on the salad plate and pushed it nearer to the pizza.

'Okay, okay. Right.' Joe put a modest amount onto his pizza plate. 'What's on the box tonight?'

'Depends what time you finish.'

'I'm nearly finished now.' Joe swilled coke around his mouth and shovelled up another forkful of food.

'I meant your homework.'

'Jeez, Dad, not yet.'

'You must. You'd better get down to it straight away. Before you get tired. Give it your best. It's a menace, but you have to swot if you want to get on, get a good job...'

'... and all that,' Joe sighed as he lifted a bulging school bag.

Martin watched him trudge upstairs. The single bedroom was filled mostly by the desk, the pile of textbooks, the jar of mangled pens. What was he urging his son towards? What "good job" wouldn't be taken over by robots by the time Joe got out of uni? In five years' time, robots would be doing the sort of job the lad could get now, just as three apps had entirely obliterated the need for the skills he himself once offered.

'Give it a good hour,' he called after Joe. 'Then leave it. The second part of *The Lone Detective*'s on at eight-thirty.'

He returned to the living room, opened his laptop and checked the latest job notifications from *Tiger Leads*. He might be better leaving his humiliating demoted job. Perhaps it was time he side-stepped, mentored young recruits, retrained in something, joined the gym, stopped watching the telly.

Only…

There was an episode of *Naked Attraction* he hadn't seen. He closed the curtains. He closed the door. This episode would just fit it in before *The Lone Detective* started and he released Joe from study.

A FORM OF PATIENCE

My feet had been long and straight, longer than all my peers, striding in front of me, purposeful, showing my planned way ahead to a bright future. Now they turned to the sides. The big toes of each foot had been decapitated, yes the heads of the largest little men gone, unsaved. The muscles of my calves were damaged, my knees, not my knees any more, but plastic replacements. That's what the car accident did to me.

In hospital, all the pain, the indignity of being immobile, bed-panned and bed-bathed by nurses you wouldn't have taken even your tie off for, relegated to a dormitory of the damaged. *One Leg Ward* we called it. Lucky, lucky me owning two.

After hospital, it was rehabilitation, learning to stand, to balance. More, I was changed; and I hadn't willed any of this.

My wife was the soul of sympathy, and saintly with it. 'Your face hasn't changed one bit, darling.' She didn't see what was behind my face.

At first, I hobbled along, the stick on my right hand, my wife on my left, where she belonged. Then I was 'rehabilitated' enough to walk on my own. I walked around the garden, round and round. I couldn't pull out any weeds or move a pot. I was too unbalanced to bend.

I got better, dispensed with the stick. I improved.

'You need your work, darling. You'll feel far less tetchy.'

I made a point of walking to work to show my independence. I attracted stares as I lurched from side to side, I knew that. My line manager told me to take it slowly. They'd be pleased with whatever I could contribute, no rush.

No—because a smarmy upstart was sitting in my place, "holding the fort".

They were not going to see me in loose elasticated trousers and a soft shirt; I wore my dark suit, a white shirt. On the fourth floor of Egress Enterprises, one colleague after the other offered commiserations and encouragement. That sympathy, passed out in the boardroom and by the water dispenser, didn't compensate for the muffled giggles in the corridors. I heard what they called me – the penguin.

I waddled home.

'How did it go, darling? A nice beef casserole coming up. Why don't you change into your comfortable clothes.' She passed me my slippers.

The mall entrance stood conveniently beside Egress Enterprises. Next day, I waddled in after work, perused the counters of gift shops, *Your Perfect Home inc.*, even the toy shop.

At home, I placed a pair of penguin book-stops to support the wife's row of wartime romances. I filled the glass-fronted cabinets with my glass and ceramic penguins.

'Oh, you've got a new interest!' My wife relies on encouragement.

'Yes.'

The next day, Waterstones and Bookends revealed their penguin literature, as well as picturesque penguin books featuring their daily lives in water, out of water, with eggs, in pairs, in colonies, on ice caps.

The shelved wartime romances had to give way for penguin books. 'Oh! Well, just for now, dear.'

Day by day, I moved the knick-knacks from shelves and mantlepiece, replacing my wife's treasures with plastic penguins in graded sizes, and soft fluffy penguins on the window sill.

'Oh, so sweet!'

'Yes. Have a cuddle.' I passed her the largest, the size of a baby.

Good photographs of penguins are not hard to find. I had them framed to line our walls and bought a fine oil painting of a king penguin. We could admire it every night and morning. It hung opposite the foot of our bed,

On Saturdays, when she asked where I'd like to go, I said, 'The antique rooms'.

Over four levels, dealers displayed wares of all kinds. She was patient while I surveyed the dealers' stalls, not hearing as I muttered to each, 'Any penguin items?'

I came home with an ashtray, a penguin as its handle, a childrens' rocking chair, a penguin forming the seat and back so the kid could feel he was sitting on a penguin's lap, and some napkins with penguins embroidered at the corners.

My wife unwrapped them, her brow wrinkled. 'You don't smoke, darling, and we always have paper serviettes.'

'Times change,' I said darkly.

'And we don't have any children.'

(And we wouldn't be having any now, would we.)

'But you can look at it. Isn't it charming?' I rocked the penguin chair to and fro.

Amazon and eBay proved rich sources of penguin material. The parcels were a real uplift when I got home after work where I assisted former colleagues, "as best you can."

My wife asked if I'd be all right while she visited her mother. 'You could come, too.' I assessed her degree of enthusiasm.

'No. She wouldn't want to see me like this.'

'I don't like to leave you alone. You won't be morose, will you?'

'I'll be fine. I'll do some chores.'

House to myself, I changed the bed, put the duvet in one of those vacuum bags that suck the life out of things and deform their appearance. I remade it with my new softee blankets adorned all over with penguins.

I opened another Amazon package. The boutique bathroom fittings were a delight: hard and shiny penguins adorned the wall hooks, the toilet brush and stand, the toilet roll holder and, yes, I'd even found penguin toilet paper. She could wipe her bum on penguins.

When my wife returned, she tried to show pleasure. 'You've done so much.' As she brought a tray of tea with the penguin biscuits, her voice wavered a little, 'but I think we have enough penguin stuff now.'

'Enough for who,' I said. It was a rhetorical question, and it should have been "whom".

The atmosphere at home hovered from tense to tempestuous, even when I bought her a present of gloves with penguin fingers.

I bided my time, penguin books on my lap, documentaries about the life of penguins on the telly.

Sundays, I proposed further zoo visits to watch the penguin show, to talk to the keeper at the penguin pool and check on the penguin I'd persuaded my wife to adopt. She was unreasonably reluctant to also donate a monthly amount to the Penguin Preservation Society, but eventually caved in.

She was so patient with me. Too patient.

One evening over dinner, I wiped my mouth on a corner of the penguin-edged napkin and announced, 'I've decided to change my name by deed poll.'

'But what's wrong with Sidney?'

'Nothing. I will keep Sidney. Sidney Penguin. Mr Penguin.'

Her gasp came near to a scream, then turned into one. 'You can't, caaaan't.'

I put an arm around her waist, probably for the last time. 'But you'd be Mrs Penguin, my Mrs Penguin, Delia Penguin.'

'Oh.o.o.o.o,' she wailed as she rushed upstairs to pack her case, and when she struggled down with it, 'That's it, Sidney! You've taken this obsession too far. I can't stay married to you anymore.'

'Penguins mate for life,' I stated.

She shouted something not even a penguin should hear.

I stayed seated until the front door shut behind her, even when she tripped over a trailing belt from her case and fell on her face. I could hear the wail and kerfuffle but it wasn't my business now. The car drove away; cough, choke, zoom.

Delia was gone.

At last.

Then I removed all the penguinalia, the evidence. It would go to the local Children's Home or some obsessive on eBay.

Come the divorce proceedings, it will look grim that she walked out on a husband still recovering from a very nasty car accident, a one-hundred-per-cent fault accident: the accident caused by someone's dreadful driving—hers.

"Only her husband hurt," reported the newspaper.

"Only?" And she was not even fined.

Did Delia really think she would get away scot-free?

Let's just see how she gets away without me…

SUCCESS AND SUCCESSOR

Delia Crossingham and *Lehmann P. Grant*! You might well be impressed. Read on.

After Sidney (what a drama), I concentrated on my career. It had been on hold while he recuperated.

The penguin episode allowed me to drop the sympathetic wife stuff. I pulled myself together. You can't feel guilty forever, and divorce is a business arrangement like any other, if you take the emotion out. I did. Anyway, Sidney was busy with his *retribution*.

I moved to the East coast. Easier to gain promotion there. It wasn't long before we had a team development thing, a management weekend. There were several hotels in the seaside town, the Imperial accommodating the bulk of our delegates. I chose the Waverley. Safe, comfortable. It was where the company had arranged the catering.

And the Waverley was where I met him. Not that I noticed him at first, he was just one of many suits there. He came and stood opposite me. I was alternately sipping coffee and nibbling a standard shortbread biscuit that leaked crumbs onto the glass-topped table.

'Are you staying here?' he said.

'No.' I didn't even look up. 'Some of us have to be over the road, overflow rooms. It's not as good.' I spoke dismissively, to discourage him.

'I come here, often,' he said.

Then I looked up and realised my mistake. It wasn't one of my insurance group colleagues. This was a stranger, nothing to do with the conference at all. How best to retract from any readiness I might have shown to accept his approach?

His rather sad dark eyes and rubbery chin were uncomfortably close as he leaned across my table. 'Shall I sit down?' and he did.

I didn't show pleasure. 'I'm sorry. I thought you were one of us. I see now I haven't met you. I'm here on business.' Would it be too brutal to rise and move off straight away?

'Sure. Never mind. There's later. When do you finish?' He stretched out a hairless hand, veins splayed, fingers strong. 'Lehmann Grant.'

Handshaking was safe enough. I complied. As it was, our next session was imminent. 'I'm Delia Crossingham. Sorry, I must get on to our 11.15 session.' The coffee hadn't been particularly good. The remains slopped around, some in the saucer as I moved my chair and stood. 'Bye.'

I went to join three of the suits I knew fairly well, one of them acknowledging me with a quick up and down of his eyebrows.

The stranger's voice sounded behind me. He'd followed. Damn. 'Ah, Delia's with you lot, is she?' It looked as if he knew at least one of these suits, and now he'd pretend he knew me. I wasn't going to play. Best to take off to the Ladies. At least he couldn't follow me there.

I came out flanked by two female colleagues. I kept my eye focussed on them, pretending a fascination with a point they'd made in our previous session. I deliberately didn't look around but strode straight across the road and into the conference, making sure I was directly between the other two. They were junior to me, so pleased enough to have my attention.

After the session, my line manager took my arm. 'Lucky you, Delia. I see you've taken the eye of Lehmann Grant.'

'Have I?' I said, nonchalantly. 'Should I care?'

'You should care. He's sunk half a million into our company. He lives between an apartment in Hans Crescent, Kensington and a villa in Sandbanks, Poole. Widowed last year, he hasn't been accompanied by a female under sixty, since. I don't deny, it would benefit our firm to have you closely linked to Lehmann but if you're even half aware, you must see how it would benefit you.'

Was he thinking of the retribution Sidney was about to take? I'd only told one person about the penguin business and the divorce settlement. It was lunch-time. I smiled and joined my team, letting out my breath slowly.

After the day's work, said Mr Grant appeared and invited me to dinner. I didn't refuse. It was nearly six months since my separation. A certain amount of humiliation and negative vibes from mutual friends had followed. Some of them said what I'd done to Sidney was unforgivable: first the life-changing accident, and then abandoning him. Who would understand assault by penguin! Ah yes, some romantic novelty and blue-eyed gazing, wouldn't come amiss. Work had become increasingly important, but underneath my professional carapace, I knew I was pretending to myself. After months of running round in circles after damaged Sidney, what I really wanted was a pandering to *my* needs.

What Lehmann offered was sophisticated socializing. This started with our first meal out. The dinner was exceptional. I risked asking Lehmann why on earth he'd upended his arrangements to take out a woman he didn't even know?

'I didn't know you yesterday, but I knew of you. And now I've met you, I will grow to know you.' It sounded like a poem. I couldn't follow his motivation or reasoning. Shouldn't I just accept my good luck?

He told me, sadly he had lost his wife, Margaret, to cancer just over a year before. 'It was a terrible time, watching her fade away. I don't want to think about it again. It's time for me to start a second life.'

Of course. How sensible. Lehmann was a practical man who had grieved and got over his loss. I would bring fresh air, perhaps that second life.

The following weeks flew by in a whirl of meetings, partings, dinners, week-end forays.

We hadn't slept together. I was pleased about that. It suggested respect and a real commitment to a relationship not powered by pure lust.

Lehmann had many business commitments. I had to keep on at work. But my mind was almost always on him and our next meeting. He said his mind was always on me. It seemed he'd recovered from his wife's death. He showed every sign of being fully into me. He'd surely be longing to cement the romance in the usual way. We hadn't been in London or near Poole, as it happened, so he hadn't shown me either of his homes.

I didn't want to think about it, but with his assets, Lehmann could acquire pure up-market sex served at any time he wanted and without entanglement. He would have minders to preserve his privacy, his business interests, his reputation.

I was wrong. He wasn't into casual sex. Several interested colleagues fed me that titbit. One night after dinner, Lehmann took me home. He had been in my flat for coffee; at times he'd collected me for the theatre, but only remained inside briefly. This time he lingered.

Putting his hands gently either side of my waist, he said, 'Delia, we've been going out together for five weeks now. I was calculating the time while we were eating dessert. I want to sleep with you. I'd adore making love to you, but the moment has to be just right. What do you say? I haven't rushed you, have I, but are you ready to love me equally?'

How charming! How could I refuse? I put my arms around him and we stayed in that gentle but intense hug for some time. Then we sat down together to plan. It was even more exciting choosing the actual moment when we'd make love, discussing possibilities with Lehmann. No man had ever given me such consideration before. How I resented, now, the fumblings and fallings-upon that had happened in my pre-marital years, the breathy kisses and forceful pelvic thrusts leading to rushed removal of clothes and an untidy coupling before an uneasy night's sleep.

We chose to go to a riverside hotel for this significant coupling, a hotel that offered a garden, scenic views, delicate décor and reportedly luxurious beds.

The day came, even the sun shone. We had dinner, walked in the garden, and then took a leisurely stroll around the hotel, which had several beautifully apportioned public rooms. Eventually, drawing out the pleasure, we went to our bedroom. I stood before him and looked him all over, savouring those auspicious moments between friendship and total commitment.

'Delia,' he said, as he stroked my hair. 'You know, you're really beautiful.'

'No,' I smiled, always realistic. 'I'm not. But it's wonderful if I am in your eyes.'

'You are indeed. I am so lucky to have found you.' For a moment I imagined Lehmann searching among lines of young women for exactly the right one, just as he searched pages of shares before selecting the one he'd invest in.

It wasn't his riches, his luxurious life-style that had made me commit to him but the simple draw that every woman responds to: the sense she possesses the true love of a man she's attracted to.

And he was attractive. The way he dressed, for a start. The suits hung perfectly down his length; the polo shirts and jeans or chinos always coordinated perfectly, the colours complementing his skin and near bronze hair. His grey eyes, crinkled lines around them, expressed such warmth and understanding. The feel of his strong arms around me, his firm but gentle kisses, urging but never urgent.

We took our time undressing and getting into bed. I luxuriated in the silken sheets that were sure to extend all the pleasure I was about to experience.

Lehmann was so sure in his movements, yet not arrogant. His eyes never left me and I was eager to begin the love-making.

I don't think I'll ever feel such intense pleasure again, I thought, as I stroked him and gave myself to him.

The love-making was perfect, and as Lehmann reached his climax, eyes screwed tight with ecstasy, I believed I had never given a man greater pleasure than this. I thrust my pelvis harder and harder into him, my truest act of devotion.

He groaned and let out a huge sigh, 'Margaret, oh Margaret.'

My body stilled, and I sensed him sensing this. He'd actually forgotten who I was in the intensity of 'our' love-making!

I was silent and moved not a muscle. His breath was absent; he wasn't breathing. Then he rolled slowly away and off me. There was a pause, heavy with my silence. 'So very sorry,' he muttered.

I didn't change my position, flattened into the mattress by his actions. I said nothing, would say nothing, there was nothing to say. In the dreadful quiet, my thoughts ran over the entire course of our affair, our honeymoon as I had imagined it. Every loving movement, every time he had sighed before kissing me, eyes focused on my lips themselves, he hadn't been with me, none of it was for me. When his eyes searched mine, he was looking for Margaret, Margaret. What qualities had kept this Lehmann Grant an eternal lover?

I had never seen a photograph of her. Probably his two homes were full of them. Now I dreaded she was some look-alike, that I would always walk around in her shadow, never in her shoes. Lehmann had been looking at me all these weeks, and seeing Margaret.

We must have slept a little. I dared not move for fear of what he would do, say, as I left him. I couldn't risk any form of response. But the semen on me had dried and was stretching the thin skin of my thighs. The urge to wash everything away was too intense to delay. I slid swiftly to the bathroom, giving him no chance to put out his loving hand and stroking fingers.

Behind the locked door, I stayed in a warm bath for as long as I could, without risking interruption. I stretched out, striving to gain comfort from warm water alone.

My clothes were still on the bathroom stool. I dried myself and put them on. The steamy mirror displayed a parody of the self I had imagined. Here I was, Delia Crossingham, ready for work again.

I stiffened myself to steal back into the bedroom, pick up my bag and make my sad announcement, the devastating news that our relationship was over. I must prepare myself to argue against his excuses, apologies and desperate pleas for another chance. I drew a deep breath and opened the door. 'Lehmann, I have to go.'

The room was empty, the bed neat. Upon it, a note. 'So sorry.' He hadn't even added my name.

Of all voices, Sidney's came to mind. "Penguins mate for life."

PRU ABOUT MEN

You see! Who'd have predicted a man like that would mess things up? How curious these men are! And I don't exclude my own line of sons. Just as we have men taped as either losers and needy, or rich and predatory, poor Delia had to come across the one man who trashed our assumptions.

Lehmann Grant, with enough money to recompense an entire coastal village for their recent flood damage, was attracted to Delia ... to an extent. He had everything a man could desire in the corporate world, yet was unreasonably demanding in the corporal one. You can't insist on past love just because you want the unattainable. Margaret, sad to say, had died. With all the live women available to him, Lehmann Grant had to yearn for someone who no longer existed. Typical. Give a man wealth, success, position, power, attractiveness and he wants the one thing he can't have.

Now, I don't have that frustration, but having struggled through a multiplicity of motherhood plus management of marriage on the side, years of it, I find myself landed with a husband who seems suddenly to have lost it.

You'll see...

THE KEY QUESTION

I'm in the kitchen, still in my dressing gown. We've had our breakfast and now I'm washing the dishes. He's behind me, not doing anything.

He speaks. 'Where were you last night?'

I stare at him, but he's serious. I humour him. 'I was with you.'

'No.'

'Yes.' My eyes widen until the rims are dry and hard. That usually quietens people. 'We ate poached salmon and new potatoes with spinach. You left the spinach, judging it bitter. Afterwards, we laughed over the orange sorbet, remembering that time Delores DelMonte dropped her dessert down her satin bodice, previously white. We went to bed early.' I lean back against the island, triumphant.

We've always enjoyed contests, both of us clever; in the case of a crossword or conundrum, we vie over who provided the most perfect answer. I'm good on detail; he's better at concepts.

He rocks on his heels, hand on chin, then leans forward, portraying the sort of person owning the most point. 'But where were you last night?'

'Here.' This is funny, then confusing. Really! Doesn't he believe me? This is becoming a pattern. I go up to the bedroom. Time to get dressed.

'Where are you going?' he challenges each day. 'Where have you been?'

I let him keep track of me, show diary entries, invite him to telephone my office, dentist, hairdresser. Returning home, I leave my mobile by his suspicious hands that weave around it, tip-tapping, tick-tacking. I let him open every message. 'Read them,' I say. 'All about work. See?'

'Where were you last night?'

I try not to let my eyebrows arch too high. 'You remember. I came home from badminton, took a shower, watched that film with you, the one you love, the one about the Englishwoman sailing down the Nile.'

He narrows his eyes, blue in a yellowish sea.

I play with him, saying it back: 'And where were you, darling?'

'Don't be silly,' he says, crossly. 'You know I was here.'

That night we watch a film, laugh, lie back on the sofa, drinks in hand. Later, hand in hand we move to the stairs. We go to bed, sleep.

And the next day, I keep to my normal routine for a Wednesday. Shopping, library, coffee with my discussion group. I get home at tea-time, ready to phone our daughter (all the rest of the brood are sons). 'I'm ho-ome.'

He's hovering in the hall. It's still, 'Where were you last night?'

'Here!' I laugh.

But when he says it every night, before the answer, after the answer, I decide to bring our doctor neighbour in, a friend of nine years' standing. He sits us both down, has tea with us. We've been on foursomes to the theatre in the past, the not too distant past. He mentions one of those plays.

My husband snorts, 'Never seen it. I don't like Miller's plays.'

'I'm sure you said you enjoyed it, at the time.'

'No. Couldn't have done. Wasn't there.'

Our cups are drained. I take the tea-tray to the door but stay there, listening.

'Do you know what day it is?' the doctor asks my husband.

'An auspicious day, I suspect.'

'Can you tell me what two and two makes, and who is the prime minister?'

My husband stands up. He'd be a full head taller than us, than everyone, if he stood straight, as he did when we were parents of a brood of noisy boys... and a girl.

'Aha!' He wags a wavering finger at me. 'I can put two and two together!'

I frown. What on earth now?

He points at me. 'Wait right there!'

Then he turns to the doctor. 'The prime minister. *Who is the prime minister?* Who *is* he, indeed! What sort of man is he?' A grim smile comes to his face, a knowing one.

He wags his finger. Points it at me.

He strides towards our neighbour and squares up to him. 'You can tell the prime minister, the husband *knows.* So it's better he resigns. Right now! Where was *he* last night? You answer me that.'

LIFE BEFORE CHAIRS

The pile of unrepaired shoes lay upturned at the bottom of the stairs: applicants awaiting Ernest's attention. He would look at them *later*. He was near to finishing re-heeling the brown suede bootees of a lady with size ten feet and a girth to match. Mr Shoe and Key had gone for an early lunch.

Ernest cast his eyes (one did have a slight cast) upon the white overall with its checked lapels, and embroidered name on the pocket. It lay over the back of the only chair. Ernest liked to slip it on, look at his reflection in the glass door and imagine owning one like this. His own overall was brown with no embroidered writing. The lapels were plain. Wearing it made him ordinary. He turned his eyes away from temptation because he needed a quick exit to attend a lecture. The Institute had such interesting lectures, sometimes at lunchtime, like today. Ernest would definitely attend. Nearly lunchtime, now. No time for white overalls, no time to sample being Mr Shoe and Key.

Mr Shoe and Key had said the lecture title was *Life Before Chairs*. Ernest couldn't imagine such a life. Chairs seemed so necessary. When you could avoid standing, you sat down. Normally on a chair. He looked at their one shop chair. Elderly customers often used it. And once, a fallen woman, brought inside to await the ambulance, had sat on this chair and bent her head between her knees. She couldn't have done that, standing.

He tidied the scraps of leather from his bench. What was Life like before chairs? That question was interrupted by the telephone ringing. After a moment's shock, Ernest remembered his responsibility and lifted the receiver. He swallowed. 'Mr Shoe and Key, but Mr Shoe and Key isn't here at present. Call back after lunch,' he suggested helpfully. As usual, he had to say this all twice. People never seemed to listen properly, always saying *What?* He replaced the receiver. It had always been the same. In his schooldays, when he'd spoken, children answered him in a funny voice while grinning around at everyone else. 'I'm Ern-etht,' they would say, and then they'd all laugh, because of course they weren't.

It wasn't clear to him why his parents called him Ernest since other people were called, say, Rob for Robert and Drew for Andrew, but no-one could call him 'Ern', like that vase you put dead peoples' ashes into (only probably not all of a person got in) or 'Nest', like a bird's home. That would be silly. The other children didn't call him Ern or Nest or even Ernest. They called him something different, and it wasn't even his name. As for teachers, after he'd been telling them everything about something he knew, like gear levers, they did sometimes say with a smile, 'You really are earnest.' So they knew, and he would reply, 'Yes I am.'

He enjoyed school lessons, especially when these were facts or puzzles, but he often failed exams. The problem was the teachers' use of multiple choice, and only wanting ticks or crosses instead of the answers Ernest carefully wrote. He followed his father's advice, "It's important not to be caught out in Life. Always consider all possible answers to problems."

Exams were for catching you out. Ernest was careful. For instance: **Tick the right box.**

5 a) Two times three is: *eight, five, or six*?

Ernest would tick each box then add a question mark before writing: '*Eight* might be correct if you turned one 3 backwards and joined it face to face with the second 3; *Five* would be correct if the numbers were in a line and you moved your finger twice past 3. *Six* is a trick, pretending to be multiplication, but actually 2 times 3 is NOT 6, only 6 can be 6. This should say *equals* 6 if this is a multiplication sum.' He'd put down his pencil and smile around, knowing most of the class were being caught out.

Then he would go onto 5 b) and give this the same earnest attention. He would run out of time, and at the end of the examination have five answers completed when the other children had thirty-five. Sadly, teachers liked ticked boxes. They far preferred them to what Ernest had to say.

'Just stick to the instructions, Ernest,' they'd sigh. 'For each answer, one number, that's all.'

The situation was worse for subjects that did require words. Discussing each set question fully meant that Ernest was still deep in *Compare* before ever reaching *Contrast*.

At the end of his school years, with no certificates, he had to take what his parents called an ordinary job. His speech not understood, and his written work undervalued, made getting a job difficult. His father spoke highly of private enterprise, so when Ernest saw a job advertised in a small shop window – visibly not a chain store – he walked in. The welcoming smell of leather, hot glue and metal filings and the sight of shining keys dangling in a row, assured Ernest of pleasure to come.

Although Mr Shoe and Key had a two-day beard and the kind of teeth that tore at meat in an intimidating way, Ernest applied to work at *Mr Shoe and Key* because stating exactly what you did was his ideal. His father called round later, and afterwards Mr Shoe and Key was exceptionally nice and took on Ernest as his assistant.

The shop name, *Mr Shoe and Key*, pleased Ernest greatly. Mr Shoe and Key worked only upon shoes and keys. A woman had come in last week and asked Ernest if they took dry cleaning! He had been polite. 'This is a shoe repair and key cutting shop, Madam.' He was going to point to the sign, but not everyone can read, he recalled from school. Ernest did like the fact that the owner had called the shop after himself. He always called him Mr Shoe and Key, never by his first name, which was Stanley.

He learned how to repair shoes first. The shoes huddled shabbily in ones and twos and, when he and Mr Shoe and Key were busy, in piles so high they had to be stacked on the narrow stairs that led to a dark and dusty attic. Ernest never went further than the first three stairs because of spiders, but he could see all the way up to the high sloping windows, dark with debris and decorated by cobwebs.

How enticing were the shining keys dangling so neatly on their hooks, one behind the other! They looked identical, but each was destined to be different and secret to its own lock. Creating this difference required skill. The key must be placed just so, before the machine whirred; an exciting task. Afterwards, the hand filing began. This required absolute precision; sadly, a process proving not to be Ernest's forté. He was much safer with shoes and, by general agreement, his working area was behind the bench with its cast iron last, awl stitcher, dowels, hot glue, and hoof knife.

'You major in repairing shoes, Ernest. Right?' said Mr Shoe and Key.

And when they were both present in the shop, Ernest confined himself to the very varied problems of shoe repair: leather or rubber re-soling, winter grips, replacing heels, re-welting and welt stitching, patching, stretching, adding segs and toe tips, and for the boots, repairing chaps, adding pulls and sliders. These details were enough to test the skill of a saint. He felt fulfilled.

There was one downer. His plain overall. This was an issue that rankled. Ernest's father believed firmly in equality, and a brown overall demonstrated to everyone coming to the shop that Ernest was not the equal of Mr Shoe and Key. If one of them was to take a break and sit on the chair, it would not be Ernest.

Life before chairs must have been uncomfortable, Ernest considered, having to sit on rocks or the hard ground, or perhaps there was some early seating device which was not a chair and of which Ernest had never learned.

Life Before Chairs. After the moment of birth, not much of life passes before a person sits on chairs, rather than laps. Babies have high chairs and push chairs. These are called buggies now, but once upon a time they were named perambulators, and later this name was shortened to prams. Ernest knew things like this even though he didn't have babies and wouldn't be having any, probably, unless he got married, and he hadn't got a girl-friend yet. He had looked at girls. His mother had always expressed the hope he would go out with a nice girl. But how could anyone tell if a girl was nice by looking at her?

Another thought. Did the lecture title mean *LIFE! before chairs*, suggesting we spend too much time sitting around looking at or after Life, instead of living it?

It was four minutes thirteen seconds before one o'clock, almost time for Ernest to lock up. His breath came a little short as he anticipated what was to come. It wasn't far to go: a ten minutes struggle uphill; a journey from knowing nothing to knowing everything about today's lecture. He would re-deliver it to whoever sat beside him on the forty-minute bus ride home tonight.

He completed his task on the brown suede bootees by tying an elaborate bow with each lace, then, for fun, knotting these together, before placing them in a brown paper bag. He was just writing the label when the doorbell jangled, announcing a new customer.

'It's only simple,' the man said. 'Just stick back this sole; it's tripping me up. Can you have it ready by two?'

'Not two,' said Ernest, 'because I'm going to the lecture *Life Before Chairs.*'

'Is that so?'

'It *is* so. And I have to walk to the Institute at the top of the hill. So I doubt if I can look at your sole before three. In fact,' he looked up at the clock with its nice big numbers, 'I must shut up right now as it is a second before one o'clock.'

He ushered the customer out, locked the door with the three dull keys and turned the sign to *Closed*. He wound his grey and maroon scarf round his lengthy neck before using the urinal and loping out of the back door. Remembering his propensity to bump into things, even people, he adjusted his pace to a dignified step.

The walk to the Institute was too far to stop for any lunch. Ernest didn't mind because he had eaten bacon and egg at his morning break. He treated himself like this from time to time and was careful not to be caught out. There were three cafés, one of which promised 'English fry-up' but when he'd ordered bacon and egg, the plate had come back swimming in beans, with the egg on one side and the bacon plopped in the middle. He never went there again. The second café had "Eggs and Bacon" on the menu. This being the wrong order, Ernest avoided the place. At the third café, to which he was now loyal, they knew 'bacon and egg' meant a rasher of bacon either side of the plate with the egg neatly in the middle, like a child with its parents supervising. They knew to ask if he wanted extras, such as beans or half a tomato, and if he did, to put them on a side plate, separately.

He would have nothing to eat now. Even if he had been starving hungry, missing lunch would be a small price to pay for the benefit of hearing such an interesting lecture. Last time Ernest attended one, it had been about finding stegosaurus remains in the muds of a remote Lithuanian estuary. He had touched the actual bones and identified them from the chart displayed on the screen. He'd sat in the front row because the time before that, a lecture about a bloody rebellion in Patagonia, a very large woman had blocked his view, especially when she nodded. She clearly felt passionately about that powerful anarcho-syndicalist labour union in 1921 but now Ernest couldn't, because of not seeing the illustrations. It was so vital to see what was lectured about!

Life Before Chairs must refer to a time long ago, and could be true of Patagonia as much as England (or should he say Great Britain as his grandparents amusingly called it, pointing to the little pink bits on their ancient map) though Ernest couldn't say whether *Before Chairs* would be as long ago as the time of a stegosaurus, but it must be well *Before Christ*, if you believed bible illustrations.

During his reverie, he failed to notice a girl in front of him as he crossed the road. He collided and nearly tripped her up. 'I'm sorry,' is what he said, but somehow it sounded different. She giggled as she removed her hands from his corduroy trousers she'd grabbed in preference to falling across the kerb. She might have been a nice girl but he couldn't help his dismay at the worn-down heels of her red court shoes. Four pounds fifty, it would have cost her, for a neat repair.

The disentanglement with the girl, nice or not, brought Ernest up short in front of the furniture store where a whole row of chairs stood in the window. It was like a sign. Here he was *standing before chairs.* Like a lecturer! Could the lecture be about lecturers? They were always before chairs, lots of them. They might spend their life, or most of it, before chairs. Unless... Ernest hurried into the store. There could be another explanation. He looked at several of the chairs closely.

'Can I help?' asked a young man sporting a greasy tuft of fore hair and cheap black shoes with carelessly knotted laces.

'Yes. Is much work required to make these chairs?'

'Er— I'm sorry?'

Ernest repeated his sentence. It was important to be tolerant.

'Oh. No, not these, they're flat pack. But there would be work involved in making this one.' He pointed to an ornate saddle chair. 'This is handmade.'

'So the – carpenter – would have spent much time before it?'

'Eh?'

'Kneeling before this chair. *He'd have spent much time before the chair.*' Ernest took especial trouble to make himself clear since the young man's *"Eh"* rather than a clear statement of hours and minutes, the *obvious* format for the answer, indicated he was not too bright.

'I suppose so. You taking it up as a hobby?'

'No. I am just going to a lecture that may be about this very thing.'

'Oh.' The assistant's bony hands dropped to his sides. 'You didn't want to buy a chair, then?'

'No. I wanted to understand about making one.'

'Yeah? Right then.' The young man held the door open for Ernest who, striding meaningfully towards it, unfortunately tripped on a Chinese rug, knocking into a highly polished side table with its display of Wedgewood dishes. Luckily, the young man was agile and caught one in mid-flight, before sliding the table with the remaining dishes back upright.

When Ernest regained his feet, he moved to help but the young man told him not to worry, and held the door wide open again.

Losing a degree of dignity before someone less able than himself caused Ernest to quicken his pace. He walked so fast that a passer-by called crudely, 'What's the hurry, mate? Bee up your arse?' He ignored the remark. You had to accept strange suggestions in a multi-cultural society. He remembered a lecture about that.

By now, he'd decided against the lecture being about the making of chairs. He'd been told before about using his imagination too freely. Carpenters, or was it furniture-makers, did not confine themselves to chairs and the lecture specifically stated Chairs. He would soon know the answer.

The streets now converged upon a pedestrian avenue filled with window-shoppers. He took another turning at, he estimated, thirty-nine degrees to the one he stood in. This took him uphill steeply, forcing him to slow down. As he neared the Institute building, he noted a queue in front. He huffed and panted in his hurry to join it.

A large lady in a suit of reddish hue emerged from the Institute door and moved down the line, looking at people on the way. She stopped by two women standing some twenty people in front of Ernest. 'I do apologise,' she said to them. 'You will not get in. Sorry to disappoint you,' and she moved her gaze across all the rest of the queue. People in it groaned and shuffled off. They must have been friends of the women, who, after a few moments of muttered discussion, moved off too. So Ernest moved up into their place. The man in front turned round and said, 'The administrator just told those two women they wouldn't get in.'

'Yes,' said Ernest. 'Shame. Disappointing for them.'

'—so it means I'll get the last seat. No use you waiting.'

'But I've come to hear *Life Before Chairs*.'

'Sorry? Oh! Today's lecture. Too bad. As said, it's full. No more seats. But it's *Regency Man and Manners* next week. Get here early, I should.'

Ernest rushed to the Institute doors where the woman in the

suit stood ready to usher the remaining fortunates into the lecture hall. 'No more seats? Can I stand?' he asked anxiously. She shook her head, 'I'm sorry. Health and Safety.'

'No, no. *Life Before Chairs.*'

'*Stairs.* It's full now,' and she ushered the last of the queue inwards and slipped after them, shutting the door with a firm clip.

He'd have been easy about stairs, whether she meant *nothing* upstairs or *full* upstairs. The ground floor was completely acceptable, *stalls,* as they oddly called it in the theatre, like toilets with doors. But he was still outside instead of in.

Some twenty-four minutes elapsed, during which Ernest paced around the building, leant an ear against the back wall, from which no sound emanated. He then stood well back to scan the upper walls in the hope of an open window from which he might catch some escaping words of wisdom.

Having no luck, he investigated the far side of the Institute, a sunless alley between the backs of several tall buildings and filled with discarded newspaper, plastic bottles, cigarette stubs and worse. Spotting a twisty fire escape with a door, a touch ajar, at the first floor level, Ernest put a foot on the first step, hesitating because of the twists. His lower legs were inclined to trip - indeed had done so twice in the last two hours - and the stairs were narrow. However, he might be able to hear the lecture if that fire door proved to be at the back of the lecture hall; perhaps even catch a glimpse of Professor Gimp giving it.

'And what would you be about, Sunshine?' A sturdy community policeman had followed Ernest with interest.

He started. 'I had hoped to be at the lecture.'

'Oh yes? The front door is around at the front, surprisingly. Let's go. You first.'

Ernest removed his foot from the iron stairs and wiped it thoroughly clean of grime on the tufts of grass poking between the paving stones.

'Like *now*,' the officer encouraged him.

They stepped carefully in single file, avoiding the worst of the debris in the alley and emerged into the light of the side road.

The officer's attention was then caught by a couple of bundles in a garage entrance. A cloth cap held coins, a line of packets behind it, all guarded by a long and lean dog of doubtful lineage. Ernest thought it wise to move off, even though this meant downhill with the inevitable climb back when the officer was well out of the way.

And indeed by the time all this was achieved and Ernest once again approached the Institute, the lecture had just ended. The audience was filtering out, led by a large man in a hurry.

'What did you learn?' Ernest asked breathlessly before he was almost knocked aside by the man's brisk buttoning-up of his cream gaberdine.

'Historiology,' he answered dismissively.

Ernest gaped after his rotund retreat. The word was unfamiliar and sounded like the sort of stumbling-within-words that happened to him on frequent occasions. He tried a young couple, bespectacled and trouser-suited, female perhaps. They stopped and explained at some length, overlaying and interrupting each other, so it was difficult to take things in.

'—the war, cultural development…'

'—over time, changes …'

'—in income,'

'—expectations, equality.'

'—how everyday artefacts give evidence of a life where …'

'—and depended on the domestic tools available as much as lower-class availability, you see.'

Ernest stammered, 'Er – *chairs*?'

One suit bent towards him with raised eyebrows. 'Not really.'

The suits looked at each other and away from Ernest, and moved off.

Well! That someone could entitle a lecture *Life Before Chairs* and then talk about something entirely different!

But it was almost time to be back at Mr Shoe and Key, where he could depend on people saying what they meant.

A growling from his mid region reminded Ernest of his sacrificed lunch. *The Ultimate Sandwich* was nearby and since he had worked nineteen minutes overtime the previous day, he decided to allow himself seventeen minutes for such a sandwich to be eaten on his return walk to work.

He couldn't be sure, after eating it quickly, whether it was truly *ultimate,* but it was cheese and tomato as printed on its wrapper. He discarded that wrapper in the correct receptacle. Bending closely to the task, he noticed his slightly smeared wrapper was a lot cleaner than the bin that now held it. But what was this?

Inside the bin, a ten-pound note lay alongside a screwed up cigarette packet. What's more, it had the imprint of a muddy sole AND the number at the top was preceded by the letters MR. It was surely intended for him, for was he not a Mr, and was that imprint not an indication of a shoe? *Mr Shoe.* This was part of what he was. Wasn't this a sign? Was it a signal that something should change? **Mr Shoe!** *Mr Shoe and Key* need not be *one* person. He did the work on the shoes, so he was Mr Shoe, and *Mr Shoe and Key* had forgotten to tell him. Mr Shoe was surely equal to Mr Key, so key changes needed to be suggested.

He loped down the hill, holding the note on high, completely forgetting his undertaking to his mother not to lope because with his long legs that looked a trifle strange. Before he reached the shop, a familiar voice behind him suggested he was a quarter of an hour late opening.

'Not late, but early. I am four minutes ahead of time. I worked nineteen minutes overtime last night,' Ernest reported as he poked the key in the lock, successful on the fourth attempt. He swivelled around when the door gave, pushing it wide open.

Mr Shoe and Key said, 'Didn't see you at the lecture.'

Ernest showed his sad face. 'No. There was no room for me.'

'I went early. My great grandad was a butler, so I had a keen interest in *Life Below Stairs.*'

'Stairs? Below!' Ernest couldn't stifle a grunt. So annoying: *behind, before, below,* they always confused him. As did *Sh* and *St* and *Ch* and *Th.* But how could *below stairs* be of interest? It was where you put the hoover, the dustpan and the box of old *Bicycles Today* and *Beanos.* Stairs? He wouldn't have liked that lecture. It was lucky there hadn't been room.

'Never mind, Ernest. Not going saved you some money.'

'Yes. Ten pounds extra, actually. Look! I have this.' He held the note up. 'See the letters, see the imprint?' He pointed them out.

Mr Shoe and Key took some time to take in the significant marks.

'Here, and here! I have just received the sign that, not only am I a key part of this shop, I am the shoe part.'

'Well, fancy that, Ernest. All that way uphill you've been, and all the way back down, and you find you're really Mr Shoe at the end of the journey. That's a kind of knowledge, I'd say.'

'Yes. Yes. Have you ever thought of me being Mr Shoe, and you Mr Key?'

'What a thought. Share the franchise? Eighty/twenty perhaps. I'd do the accounts, of course. Would your folks cough up? Put half the dosh in? Weather the load?'

'My parents' coughs? Whether... what?'

'Sorry, Ernest. What am I thinking of? Be clear, Stanley. That's what I need to remind myself. So. Will your parents stump up - give me - half the franchise cost? Are they willing to support you further?'

'Oh most certainly. They've often said they're willing to support me, whatever the challenge.'

'Good. 'Cos we could diversify with your dosh, y'know. That's what we need to make a proper return—diversification. Shoes, keys—dry cleaning, say.'

Ernest felt the sides of his mouth droop. Dry cleaning! Nothing to do with shoes or keys. 'That would stink.'

'True. It does have a strong pong. Chemicals; not good for you. All right, then, not dry cleaning. What about small upholstery repairs? Chair repair, how about that?'

'Chairs!'

'You don't fancy that? Not enough room here, perhaps? Well, what about this – it's in the latest *Franchise Review*... collars? Dog collars, cat collars, all colours, sizes, widths. Compact, on the wall, doesn't take up floor space, see. Next to the keys, hanging, bright. We like dogs, don't we, Ernest? Bit of life in here, dogs being fitted up. Not a big outlay, collars, with your dosh. What do you say?'

Ernest swallowed, his Adam's apple prominent under his chin. He fingered his ten-pound note, his Mr Shoe note. 'Mr Shoe and Key and—Collars?'

He looked at the rack of beautiful keys, their corrugated edges falling precisely in the same pattern. He imagined a row of collars, different lengths, different widths, different colours. It would take a good day to arrange them in size and intensity of hue. There was certainly room alongside the keys for them to hang. On the left would be white, ranging through yellow, orange, pink, red, blue, purple. No green, he didn't like green. At the top, short collars, ranging downwards to long ones. The widths; now how best to arrange them?

He leant against the counter, a pair of stilettos digging into his back. He was comfortable repairing soles. He'd never thought of fitting dog collars. But think—he could occupy the chair, sitting before the animal to decide upon the correct width and length. The colour would depend upon the fur. White or red for a black dog, pink for a lady's poodle, blue for a gingery daschund.

Collars. It was a new thought. *Diversification* was not a word which fell easily from his lips, if at all. Mr Key knew best about making money. He could be left to see to that. But he, Ernest, would be in charge of shoes and collars.

They would need a new shop sign above the door with two cheery cartoon men instead of one. *Mr Shoe and Collar. Mr Key.* Equals. How proud his parents would be.

Two Misters. Perhaps two chairs. His eyes focused upon the overall that Mr Key, as customers should now call him, was presently pulling on while gazing at him questioningly.

Ernest pushed his brown overall off the shoe bench and looked straight at his partner. 'I'll need a white overall with *Mr Shoe and Collar* on it, and with checked lapels.'

'You will?'

'I will.'

'*I* know you're Mr Shoe, and now *you* know. When we get the collars, you'll get a new overall but it'll say *Mr Shoe and Key*, because that's the name of the shop.'

'But it will be white?'

'As white as my teeth,' and Stanley bared his gnashers.

Ernest shut his eyes.

'Now, see that pile of shoes, BELOW STAIRS?'

Ernest hurriedly turned his attention to the many battered supplicants. They resembled his father's painting of the lost and sinned awaiting St Peter's judgement.

Stanley cajoled in a rumbling bass, 'Are you ready for them, Mr Shoe?'

Ernest was. There was the pair of shoes from the recent customer, the left revealing its loose sole ready to trip a man up, while the right displayed a badly worn underside. So like Life. He set about his noble work. Soon dogs, too, would be depending upon him for a comfortable fit and smart appearance.

'How about tonight for a little chat with your father about that franchise?' Stanley was sitting on the chair, writing in his accounts book.

Ernest inclined his head chairwards. 'I shall need to sit on something proper when I'm fitting the collars.'

'Agreed. Use the phone, let your parents know I'm coming.'

Ernest did so. They seemed pleased.

After the meeting of men, and Mother's dinner, which tonight, being Tuesday, would be chicken chunks stewed with carrots and broccoli, he might ask his father the question:

What was Life like before chairs?

WHAT WAS SAID

Jim stood at the doorway, gut over belt, determined to have it out with Brian.

'Did you tell him?' he said, as soon as Brian's apologetic eyebrows appeared around the door.

'What? Who?'

'Him,' said Jim.

'Him?' said Brian, scratching his head, patting his coat pocket, checking the door latch. 'Oh, oh, HIM? He said he was the Boss, so it was up to him to do the talking. That's what he said.'

'Is that it? The sum total?'

'Of what he said?'

Jim's voice raised half an octave, 'Of what you said to him. Of what he said to you. Of what he's going to say, since you say he said it's up to him to say it all.'

'Ugh?' said Brian, rubbing the back of his neck.

'Tell me what you said,' said Jim. 'Go on. I want to hear what you said, 'cos I reckon you chickened out and said b- all.'

Brian shook his head a little, just enough for plaster flakes to drop from his few strands of hair. 'I said ...er...'

'Yes. I want to hear what you said. Today. Now.'

'I said—well I went up to the office and he was busy.'

'Busy?' said Jim.

'On the phone,' said Brian.

'What was he saying? What did he say?'

'He said, "Bugger off, I'm on the phone."'

'And you said?' said Jim.

'I said… something like, "All right, but I want to say something after."'

'And did you?'

'When he came off the phone, I said it,' said Brian.

'Said *what* exactly? I want to know exactly what you said.'

'Er, I said, "The Men want their say, sir." That's what I said.'

'And?' said Jim.

'He said, if I wanted to say the men wanted their say then I could say it in my own time. That's what he said,' Brian said.

'It's all about what HE said. He wants it all his way.'

'You're right. That's what I say.'

'But you didn't say! We voted for you to say the things for all of us. So I'm not satisfied with what you said,' said Jim.

'I said we wanted our say.'

'But you didn't *say* our say, you twerp, so we haven't *had* our say.'

I did say we all wanted our say, Brian was going to reply but a fist in his mouth stopped him from saying anything at all for some considerable time.

THE END of Curious Men

BUT if you don't yet know the women who interrupted in this book, ME-TIME TALES awaits. Available digitally and in print, too.

AFTERWORD

I circumvented a Coda the interfering women wrote. Why should they have the last word in a book devoted to men, even if they also are curious? It was more appropriate to end this collection with a man trying to have his say. So sad that Brian failed.

You'll appreciate I have included some sober men, and at least one uplifting sentiment in this collection. I felt a need to do this. Few of my curious men are admirable, are they?

I suffer no guilt. I thoroughly enjoy creating unpopular characters. Just as some artists create a piece intending to shock but also enthral, I'd be very pleased to learn if any reader enjoyed discovering my Curious Men.

Please consider leaving a review online, however brief. Readers rarely realise how tremendously important their reviews are to an author, however short.

MY OTHER BOOKS

A RELATIVE INVASION is a trilogy set in WW2 about a fateful boyhood rivalry. Billy's personal territory is constantly invaded by his talented, manipulative cousin, Kenneth. Billy must overcome emotional neglect, wartime hardships, evacuation and disruptions as well as the psychological threat from Kenneth. But in their adolescence, the rivalry reaches an inevitable crisis.

There is also a thirties Prequel which reveals the adult characters before the two boys were born. Could the drama have been predicted back then?

A RELATIVE INVASION is available in ebook and kindle and order the paperback from your bookstore.

Book 1: Intrusion
Book 2: Infiltration
Book 3: Impact

You can have all three books in one volume, A RELATIVE INVASION - The Trilogy.

By contrast, my contemporary series of psychological suspense, **UNCOMMON RELATIONS,** features dark secrets, hidden identities, colourful characters, twists and turns of the plot, and occasional irreverent humour.

Book 1 is **Who should be forgiven** and **Book 2: What should be forgotten, while Book 3: When should they be told? is nearing completion.**

To learn more about my books, sign up for my Readers List on my website. https://rosalindminett.com. You'll receive my Newsletter for exclusive titbits...and maybe a free story.

Also, check out my blog: www.characterfulwriter.com and follow me on Bookbub.,